Charles O. Flagg, Rhode Island Agricultural experiment station

Experimental Work

conducted at the Rhode Island experiment station with the nitrate of soda

Charles O. Flagg, Rhode Island Agricultural experiment station

Experimental Work
conducted at the Rhode Island experiment station with the nitrate of soda

ISBN/EAN: 9783337380748

Printed in Europe, USA, Canada, Australia, Japan

Cover: Foto ©Andreas Hilbeck / pixelio.de

More available books at **www.hansebooks.com**

EXPERIMENTAL WORK

CONDUCTED

AT THE RHODE ISLAND EXPERIMENT STATION

WITH THE

NITRATE OF SODA,

OR

CHILE SALT-PETER

AS A

FERTILIZER ,

UPON

ACID SOILS

———

CHARLES O. FLAGG.

1898.

UNZ & CO., PRINTERS, 1 BOWLING GREEN, NEW YORK.

PREFACE.

✦✦✦

THE results of the experimental work somewhat briefly set forth in the following pages, are based upon experiments conducted by the Agricultural Experiment Station at Kingston, Rhode Island, U. S. A., upon its own grounds, and in co-operation with farmers in different sections of the state, during the years from 1890 to 1897 inclusive, when the writer was Director of the Station.

In planning the experiments, and executing the details of the work, the highest credit is due to H. J. Wheeler, Ph. D., Chemist of the Station; J. D. Towar, B. S, George M. Tucker, B. S, and J. L. Tillinghast, assistants to the Director in the Agricultural Division; B. L. Hartwell, B. S., and Chas. L. Sargent, B. S., Assistant Chemists; and Geo. E. Adams, B. S., Photographer, as well as a number of farmers who heartily supplemented the work of the Station in connection with experiments planned for their respective farms.

These experiments have formed a portion of the regular scientific work prosecuted by the Experiment Station, and a detailed account of them has been published in the Annual Reports and Bulletins issued by the Rhode Island Experiment Station while I was Director, and from which I have made frequent extracts. All the cuts used to illustrate this pamphlet have appeared in connection with the above named Reports and Bulletins, and we are indebted to the Experiment Station for the privilege of their reproduction in this connection.

As the work has progressed and results have accumulated, the superior value of *nitrate of soda* as a nitrogenous manure, especially when used upon acid soils, has become more and more evident. The numerous and somewhat intricate conditions which govern the processes of nitrification, and the natural formation of nitrates within the soil, as demonstrated in comparatively recent years by biologists, serve as scientific pointers to the reasons for its superior action upon many soils.

The intelligent reader will bear in mind that *nitrate of soda* will not do everything. Potash and phosphoric acid must be supplied, unless provided by nature, if one would harvest profitable crops, and if a soil is so acid as to render the growth of many farm crops, *especially during their infancy, impossible,* such a condition must be corrected by the use of carbonate of lime, or in some other way, before bountiful crops can be harvested.

KINGSTON, R. I , Sept. 1, 1898.   *Chas. O. Flagg.*

THE USE OF NITRATE OF SODA IN CONNECTION WITH SOME EXPERIMENTS IN RHODE ISLAND.

DURING the winter of 1889 and '90, the writer, as Director of the Rhode Island Experiment Station at Kingston, solicited the co-operation of farmers in different parts of the State in a trial of various fertilizing materials, for the following three-fold purpose:

1. That of learning, if possible, in what elements some of the soils of the State are especially lacking.

2. For testing the relative fertilizing value of nitrogen in the various nitrogen compounds, such as nitrate of soda, sulfate of ammonia and dried blood.

3. To learn something, if possible, of the probable profit or loss from large and small applications of nitrogen to the Indian corn crop.[1]

The general plan of the experiments was one adopted by Prof. W. O. Atwater in Connecticut, and the work was laid out and conducted the first year by the station chemist, Dr. H. J. Wheeler, and the remaining three years by the Director's assistant, Mr. J. D. Lowar. From twenty-one offers of land by farmers for experimental purposes, ten, which fairly represented the different sections and soils of the State, were selected. A field at the Experiment Station made the number eleven. One acre of land was used in each experiment, and so selected as to be, so far as possible, of a uniform quality. Each acre was divided into twenty plots, laid out, wherever practicable, with an unfertilized space of three feet at least between the plots and along the ends.

Plots 7 to 15 c, inclusive, were devoted to the second problem, viz., that of obtaining more information upon the relative fertilizing value

---

[1] For a detailed account of these experiments see "Third Annual Report of the R. I. Experiment Station," 1890, Part II, pages 39–107; "Fourth Annual Report" do., 1891, Part II, pages 35–81; "Fifth Annual Report" do., 1892, Part II, pages 163–198, and "Sixth Annual Report" do., 1893, Part II, pages 196–207.

of nitrogen in its various combinations, and it is in the results obtained from these plots that we are especially interested at this time. These plots received like amounts of potash and phosphoric acid, and three groups of three plots each were set apart for the testing of nitrogen in three different forms. To the first group, plots 7, 8 and 9, *nitrate of soda* was applied. The second group, plots 10, 11 and 12, received nitrogen in *sulfate of ammonia ;* and to the third group, plots 13, 14 and 15, nitrogen was applied in the form of *dried blood.*

The first plot in each series, 7, 10 and 13, was given only a "⅓ ration" of nitrogen ; the second plot in each group a "⅔ ration," or twice as much as the first, and the last plot a "full ration," or three times as much as the first.

Great care was used in applying the fertilizer evenly broadcast, to each plot, and in harrowing it in, that it should not be dragged over the boundary upon the unmanured strips, or upon the adjoining plots. White flint Indian corn was planted in hills three feet apart in the row, and the rows from 3 to 3½ feet apart, according to the width of the plots in the different fields.

As the experiment was continued on these plots from two to four years, we will briefly outline the treatment with fertilizers in the several years, before considering the individual experiments.

Mixed Minerals.

In 1890 the "mixed minerals" used upon all the plots from 7 to 15 inclusive, consisted of dissolved bone black at the rate of 350 pounds, and muriate of potash at the rate of 150 pounds per acre, at a total cost of $8.15. These materials supplied respectively 74.2 pounds of total phosphoric acid and 76.2 pounds of actual potash per acre.

In addition to the "mixed minerals," as above, nitrogen was applied to the plots in the three groups, as follows :

Nitrate of Soda Group.

				Lbs. per Acre.		Lbs Nitrogen.		Cost per Acre, including M. M. [1]
Plot	7,	⅓	ration,	-	150,	-	25.0,	-	$11 75
"	8,	⅔	"	-	300,	-	50.0,	-	15.35
"	9,	Full	"	-	450,	-	75.0,	-	18.95

[1] Mixed minerals cost $8.15 in each case.

SULFATE OF AMMONIA GROUPS.

			Lbs. per Acre.		Lbs. Nitrogen.		Cost per Acre, including M. M. [1]
Plot 10,	⅓	ration,	- 112,	-	23.5,	-	$12.07
" 11,	⅔	"	- 224,	-	47.0,	-	15.99
" 12,	Full	"	- 336,	-	70.5,	-	19.91

DRIED BLOOD GROUP.

Plot 13,	⅓	ration,	- 220,	-	25 0,	-	$12.00
" 14,	⅔	"	- 440,	-	50.0,	-	15.85
" 15,	Full	"	- 660,	-	75.0,	-	19.70

In 1891 the "mixed minerals" applied cost at the rate of $7.44 per acre. The muriate of potash was a little stronger in actual potash, and the quantity used was reduced from 150 to 130 pounds per acre, furnishing 73.1 pounds actual potash. The same weight of dissolved bone-black, 350 pounds, was used, but afterward was found to be low in phosphoric acid, so that only 52.2 pounds of total phosphoric acid were applied per acre. The same weights of nitrate of soda and dried blood were used as in 1890, but the sulfate of ammonia was increased to make the nitrogen this year fully equal to the amount in the other forms. The amounts applied to the full ration plots were as follows, and the "one-third" and "two-thirds" rations were proportional:

				Lbs. per Acre.	Lbs. Nitrogen per Acre.	Cost including M. M. [2]
Plot	9,	*Full ration Nitrate of Soda,*		450,	68.4,	$18.24
"	12,	" "	*Sulfate of Ammonia,*	348,	69.9,	20.38
"	15,	" "	*Dried Blood,*	660,	67.8,	18.99

In 1892, as potash and phosphoric acid, one or both, seemed to be deficient in the soil in most cases, and in order that there might be no uncertainty as to a sufficient supply of the mineral elements, so as profitably to use all the nitrogen supplied, the quantity of each was considerably increased. The dissolved bone-black was increased from 350 to 600 pounds, containing 93.18 pounds of total phosphoric acid per acre, and the muriate of potash from 150 pounds in 1890, and 130 in 1891 to 200 pounds, which supplied just 100 pounds of actual potash

[1] Mixed minerals cost $8.15 in each case.

[2] Mixed minerals cost $7.44.

per acre. The two together as "mixed minerals" cost \$12.20 per acre.
A little increase was also made in the nitrogen applied as follows:

		Lbs. per Acre.	Lbs. Nitrogen per Acre.	Cost including M. M. [1]
Plot 9, *Full ration Nitrate of Soda*,	480,	75.17,	\$23.48
" 12, " " *Sulfate of Ammonia*,	360,	74.92,	24.80
" 15, " " *Dried Blood*,	690,	76.04,	24.28

In 1893 the weight of "mixed minerals" applied remained the
same as in 1892, but a little difference in the chemical composition
made the amount of actual potash applied per acre, 101.3 pounds,
while the total phosphoric acid remained the same, viz., 93.18 pounds.
The cost per acre was \$12.60.

The dried blood contained less nitrogen than that obtained in previous years, and the quantity therefore had to be increased. The full
ration applications were as follows:

		Lbs. per Acre.	Lbs. Nitrogen per Acre.	Cost including M. M. [2]
Plot 9, *Full ration Nitrate of Soda*,	480,	74.40,	\$24.60
" 12, " " *Sulfate of Ammonia*,	360,	72.00,	26.10
" 15, " " *Dried Blood*,	780,	67.08,	30.15

A glance at the cost per acre of the fertilizers used will show that
each year of the experiments, *nitrate of soda* furnished the *cheapest*
source of nitrogen. The following table shows the cost per acre of
the fertilizer applied to each of the plots, the total cost per acre of the
four applications for each plot, and, finally, the total cost for each *group*
(representing three acres for four years). In each group \$121.17 of
the cost is for the "mixed minerals," potash and phosphoric acid, and
the balance of the amount represents the cost of the nitrogenous fertilizer, which for *nitrate of soda* was \$15.67 *less* than for dried blood,
and \$11.70 *less* than for sulfate of ammonia.

---

[1] Mixed minerals cost \$12.20 per acre.
[2] Mixed minerals cost \$12.60 per acre.

COST OF FERTILIZERS.

No. of Plot.	1890	1891	1892	1893	TOTALS.
		NITRATE OF SODA GROUP.			
7	$11.75	$11.04	$15.96	$16.60	$55.35
8	15.35	14.64	19.72	20.60	70.31 } $210.93
9	18.95	18.24	23.48	24.60	85.27
		SULFATE OF AMMONIA GROUP.			
10	$12.07	$11.73	$16.40	$17.10	$57.30
11	15.99	16.02	20.60	21.60	74.21 } $252.63
12	19.91	20.31	24.80	26.10	91.12
		DRIED BLOOD GROUP.			
13	$12.00	$11.29	$16.23	$18.45	$57.97
14	15.85	15.14	20.25	24.30	75.54 } $226.63
15	19.70	18.99	24.28	30.15	93.12
		MIXED MINERAL PLOTS.			
6a, 6b, 6c	$8.15	$7.44	$12.20	$12.60	$40.39

Cost of "Mixed Minerals" for each group = $40.39 × 3 = $121.17.

THE FIELD TRIALS.

I. KINGSTON, R. I.

EXPERIMENT STATION FARM.

The acre selected was a portion of the alluvial plain land at the westerly end of the farm. It had been in grass for many years and produced hardly hay enough to pay for cutting. The surface soil was only 4 or 5 inches deep, sandy loam in character, underlaid by from 2 to 4 feet of yellow loam, and there was a subsoil below that of open sand and gravel.

We give below the yields per acre of hard corn, soft corn and stover for the four years included in the experiment.

	1890			1891			1892			1893		
	HARD CORN.[1] Bus.	SOFT CORN.[2] Bus.	STOVER. Pounds.	HARD CORN. Bus.	SOFT CORN. Bus.	STOVER. Pounds.	HARD CORN. Bus.	SOFT CORN. Bus.	STOVER. Pounds.	HARD CORN. Bus.	SOFT CORN. Bus.	STOVER. Pounds.
Nitrate of Soda Group.												
Plot 7, ⅓ ration	42.14	1.79	2550	30.71	3.43	1695	37.57	5.84	2560	9.32	5.68	2400
" 8, ⅔ "	45.00	1.43	2500	37.43	1.93	2040	45.71	4.71	3230	15.15	4.72	2606
" 9, Full "	52.14	1.43	3500	46.07	2.57	2560	51.28	4.50	3595	13.07	3.97	2482
Sulfate of Ammonia Group.												
Plot 10, ⅓ ration	50.71	1.79	3000	32.78	1.50	1840	30.57	7.04	2433	6.62	4.41	1940
" 11, ⅔ "	26.42	2.86	1500	15.50	2.14	1140	7.14	4.67	907	2.52	1.44	984
" 12, Full "	15.71	2.86	1300	12.78	2.28	825	4.47	5.14	1193	1.21	2.02	624
Dried Blood Group.												
Plot 13, ⅓ ration	34.28	2.15	1750	34.07	1.57	1965	34.28	8.57	2660	9.58	3.77	2531
" 14, ⅔ "	38.57	1.43	2100	38.78	.85	1895	36.00	9.43	5320	11.14	3.21	2295
" 15, Full "	34.28	3.58	1700	27.57	3.35	1610	31.35	9.43	2645	9.47	3.88	2080

1 70 pounds of corn on the cob is reckoned as equal to a bushel of shelled corn

NOTES AND CONCLUSIONS.

1890. When the corn was about 15 inches high, the better color of the *nitrate of soda* plots began to be noticeable, and the same continued until the end of the season. The sulfate of ammonia plots, instead of improving with the advance of the season, began to take on a sickly yellow appearance, which gradually grew worse, until just before the close of the season, when a slight improvement was here and there noticeable. The greater the application of sulfate, the worse the plots appeared, and the results showed a decidedly injurious effect, the crop decreasing with the increase in the amount applied. The most important result of this experiment was the poisonous effect of

FIELD CORN (MAIZE).

Plot Nos. 29. Limed.   27. Unlimed.   25. Limed.   23. Unlimed.

Nitrate of Soda.   **Sulfate of Ammonia.**

All manured alike with Potash and Phosphoric Acid.

the increasing rations of sulfate of ammonia, and the relatively small yields from dried blood. The results were doubtless due to delayed and only partial nitrification, caused, probably, by the acidity of the soil and by the absence of carbonate of lime.

The *nitrate of soda proved much the superior source of nitrogen* on this soil, as the average of the three plots in that group showed an excess in yield over the average of the other groups.

1891. The ill effect of sulfate and ammonia continued. "Phosphoric acid was most lacking, and next to it came potash, while nitrogen gave financial profits only when used in combination with both of the other elements."

In connection with "mixed minerals" nitrogen in the form of *nitrate of soda gave far better results* than in either of the other forms; and increased applications resulted in increased yields and profits.

1892. The peculiarly injurious effects of sulfate of ammonia were again apparent. The soil had been found decidedly acid when subjected to a litmus paper test. Experiments by Dr. H. J. Wheeler have shown that an application of air slaked lime to the soil prevent the marked ill effect of applications of sulfate of ammonia.

Nitrate of soda, as a source of nitrogen, *is still much superior* to the other forms employed.

1893. The season was rather unfavorable and the yields of corn very low.

Nitrate of soda again shows its superiority by larger yields than were secured from either the sulfate of ammonia or the dried blood.

The total yields for four years in the case of each plot, and the total product from each group are shown in the following table :

SUMMARY KINGSTON EXPERIMENT, 1890-1893, INCLUSIVE.

		Plot Num-bers.	TOTAL YIELDS PER ACRE IN 4 YEARS.		
			HARD CORN. Bushel.	SOFT CORN. Bushel.	STOVER. Pounds.
Nitrate of Soda Group,	-	7	119.74	16.75	9205
		8	143.29	12.79	10376
		9	157.56	12.47	12337
	TOTALS,	......	**420.59**	**42.01**	**31918**
Sulfate of Ammonia Group,	-	10	120.68	14.74	9213
		11	51.58	11.11	4513
		12	34.17	12.30	3942
	TOTALS,	......	206.43	38.15	17668
Dried Blood Group,	- -	13	112.21	16.06	8606
		14	124.49	14.92	11810
		15	102.67	20.24	8035
	TOTALS,	......	339.37	51.22	28451

A comparison of the figures in yields per acre shows that the *nitrate of soda group exceeded* the sulfate of ammonia group, as the result of four years' crops, by 214.16 bushels of hard corn and 14250 pounds of stover, at $11.70 *less cost* for fertilizer. The *nitrate of soda group exceeded* the dried blood group, as the result of the four years' crops, by 81.22 bushels of hard corn and 3467 pounds of stover, at $15.67, *less cost* for fertilizer.

2. ABBOTT RUN, L. I.

FARM OF E. F. CROWNINSHIELD.

This experiment was in the northern part of the state, near the Massachusetts line. The soil was a very light sandy loam, and the field for many years had been used as a pasture. Two or three years previous to 1890 the thin sod had been broken up and winter rye sown. The next season buckwheat was grown and the crop turned under Fertilizer was used and Indian corn planted, which proved a failure, and "strap leaf" turnips were sown as a catch crop. In 1889 fertilizer was again applied, and a fair crop of "Hungarian" (millet) was grown. No barnyard manure was ever used on the field. The land was plowed the depth of the surface soil, about 4 or 5 inches. The plots were laid out and fertilizers applied as in the previous experiment. The yields for four years were at the rates per acre shown in Table A.

NOTES AND CONCLUSIONS.

1890. In the three groups of plots where nitrogen was added to "mixed minerals," the "most marked gains were made upon plots 7, 8 and 9, where it was applied in the form of *nitrate of soda*. But little difference is apparent in the yields upon the sulfate of ammonia and dried blood groups. It is possible that the process of nitrification was not active enough for the plant to get the benefit from the nitrogen which had been added in these forms, and that the yield would have been greater had nitrogen in the form of *nitrate of soda* been employed throughout."

Although the soil was evidently more in need of nitrogen than either phosphoric acid or potash, its application in addition to those two ("mixed minerals") was not profitable except in the form of *nitrate of soda*.

1891. "In the special nitrogen test (plots 7 to 15) we have conclusive proof of the *superior value of nitrate of soda* on this land."

	1890			1891			1892			1893		
	HARD CORN. Bus.	SOFT CORN. Bus.	STOVER. Pounds.	HARD CORN. Bus.	SOFT CORN. Bus.	STOVER. Pounds.	HARD CORN. Bus.	SOFT CORN. Bus.	STOVER. Pounds.	HARD CORN. Bus.	SOFT CORN. Bus.	STOVER. Pounds.
Nitrate of Soda Group.												
Plot 7, ⅓ ration	35.71	1.07	1200	34.28	1.71	2380	34.71	2.64	3085	28.57	1.71	1780
" 8, ⅔ "	37.14	1.43	1100	33.71	1.71	2820	39.14	2.42	3400	38.28	1.91	2235
" 9, Full "	41.43	2.14	1200	36.00	1.14	2800	40.71	2.21	3465	41.78	1.71	2255
Sulfate of Ammonia Group.												
Plot 10, ⅓ ration	23.57	4.28	850	10.00	2.28	1940	20.57	4.71	2730	11.14	5.21	1455
" 11, ⅔ "	20.00	5.00	900	26.00	3.00	2240	24.07	5.21	2650	13.50	4.28	1358
" 12, Full "	30.00	4.28	1200	15.43	2.85	2830	29.00	4.85	2430	19.07	3.57	1415
Dried Blood Group.												
Plot 13, ⅓ ration	22.86	2.14	1100	14.85	2.42	2590	18.00	1.85	3010	12.00	2.85	1560
" 14, ⅔ "	21.43	2.50	1150	20.28	2.85	2580	25.14	2.14	3290	18.71	2.28	1730
" 15, Full "	30.00	2.14	1050	25.28	2.28	2860	28.28	2.50	3245	26.85	2.14	2070

"Of the three forms of nitrogen, *nitrate of soda gave the best results.* Dried blood gave better results than sulfate of ammonia."

1892. "On all the plots where both nitrogen and phosphoric acid were applied in quantities exceeding the former applications, the yields have been materially greater and more profitable."

Nitrate of soda has again *shown its superior power.* Although sulfate of ammonia and dried blood produced about equal yields of hard corn, the dried blood gave a better yield of stover and, upon the whole, yielded a more profitable crop.

The average yield of the "mixed minerals" plots (without nitrogen) above the yield of the nothing plots was not sufficient to pay for the extra cost of fertilizers.

1893. The unfavorable season made the yields of hard corn a little lower than in 1892, and that of stover much less. *Nitrate of soda gave decidedly superior yields* over the other forms of nitrogen. The following table gives the total of the four crops for each plot and each group:

SUMMARY ABBOTT RUN EXPERIMENT,

1890-1893, INCLUSIVE.

		Plot Numbers.	TOTAL YIELDS PER ACRE IN 4 YEARS.		
			HARD CORN. Bus.	SOFT CORN. Bus.	STOVER. Pounds.
Nitrate of Soda Group,	-	7	133.27	7.13	8445
		8	148.27	6.77	9645
		9	159.92	7.20	9750
	TOTALS,	......	441.46	21.10	27840
Sulfate of Ammonia Group,	-	10	65.28	16.48	6975
		11	83.57	16.49	6545
		12	93.50	15.55	7865
	TOTALS,	......	242.35	48.52	21385
Dried Blood Group,	- -	13	67.71	9.26	8260
		14	85.56	9.77	8750
		15	113.41	9.06	9225
	TOTALS,	......	266.68	28.09	26235

In the case of each group an increase in the amount of nitrogen applied gave an increase in the total hard corn and stover obtained in four years.

The total quantity of *soft corn* obtained was much the largest in the sulfate of ammonia group. The dried blood group ranked second, and the *nitrate of soda* group produced the smallest quantity;—less than half as much as was produced by the sulfate of ammonia group. This shows a more rapid growth and early maturity on the part of the crop grown upon the *nitrate of soda*. In a northern climate, where there is a great liability to early frosts, and where a delay of a week or ten days in the time of maturity may cause serious loss, the argument for the use of nitrogen in the form of *nitrate of soda*, and of quick acting fertilizer in general, has considerable weight. The query why corn fertilized with sulfate of ammonia should be longer in maturing than when dried blood is used, seems to find its answer in the effect upon the plant, and upon the nitrification of the chemical added to an already acid soil, producing conditions which make a longer time necessary for the completion of the process of nitrification in the case of the ammonia, than is required for the whole process in the case of the dried blood.

The ⅓ ration of nitrogen in the form of *nitrate of soda*, plot 7, produced just about double the quantity of hard corn which was produced in the four years by either of the other forms of nitrogen where a ⅓ ration was used, plots 10 and 13.

The total yield for four years from all the plots in the *nitrate of soda group* stated in yields per acre, *exceeded the total yield* from all the plots in the sulfate of ammonia group by 199.11 bushels of hard corn and 6455 pounds of stover, at $11.70 *less* cost for fertilizers.

Compared with the dried blood group, the *nitrate of soda* produced at the rate of 174.78 bushels hard corn and 1605 pounds of stover *more* than the dried blood, at $15.67 *less* expense for fertilizers.

3. HOPE VALLEY, R. I.

Farm of Herbert E. Lewis.

The field in which this experiment was located had served for several years as a cow pasture, and was in a low state of fertility. The soil was sandy loam in character. The same general method of treatment was followed as in the other experiments. The yields for the four years, calculated to rates per acre, are given below :

	1890			1891			1892			1895		
	HARD CORN. Bus.	SOFT CORN. Bus.	STOVER. Pounds.	HARD CORN. Bus.	SOFT CORN. Bus.	STOVER. Pounds.	HARD CORN. Bus.	SOFT CORN. Bus.	STOVER. Pounds.	HARD CORN. Bus.	SOFT CORN. Bus.	STOVER. Pounds.
Nitrate of Soda Group.												
Plot 7, ⅓ ration...........	33.57	3.93	2675	46.00	1.21	2400	24.20	5.53	2217	22.62	4.01	1672
" 8, ⅔ "	55.00	5.36	2950	52.00	1.71	2550	36.10	3.24	2942	33.40	3.38	2190
" 9, Full "	33.57	4.64	3050	60.57	2.85	3165	35.93	2.88	2366	32.78	3.58	2556
Sulfate of Ammonia Group.												
Plot 10, ⅓ ration.....	48.21	6.07	3500	29.14	.43	2000	33.71	2.57	2050	14.24	6.00	1725
" 11, ⅔ "	60.00	5.71	4325	50.85	.57	2000	13.80	6.53	1449	5.21	4.00	1322
" 12, Full "	51.43	5.00	3600	37.71	.78	2100	17.85	7.64	2035	9.71	2.75	1021
Dried Blood Group.												
Plot 13, ⅓ ration.........	45.00	3.21	2850	42.57	.95	2050	32.48	4.17	2242	13.80	4.74	1691
" 14, ⅔ "	37.50	4.64	2900	48.53	1.57	3100	29.07	4.35	2550	22.30	4.44	2550
" 15, Full "	41.07	4.64	2900	54.00	1.21	2000	26.85	4.60	2423	21.57	4.65	2579

Notes and Conclusions.

1890. The best results were secured this season from the su - ate of ammonia group. The fact that two out of eighteen fertilized plots produced less than the yield from the two plots which received no fertilizer whatever indicates some variation in fertility. Phosphoric acid was particularly deficient in this soil, and nitrogen considerably so.

1891. *Nitrate of soda* this season gave *considerably the best yield*, dried blood occupying the second place, plots 14 and 15 surpassing last year's yield.

Sulfate of ammonia, which gave the best crop last season, is quite out-distanced by both the other forms this season.

"The application of fertilizers was accompanied by profit only when phosphoric acid was applied, and the *profit was greatest* when the full ration of nitrogen in the form of *nitrate of soda* was used in combination with phosphoric acid and potash."

1892. The yields from all the plots show a considerable reduction since the beginning of the experiment. *Nitrate of soda again gave the best crop*, with dried blood second, and sulfate of ammonia last. In the latter case, a ⅓ ration gave a larger yield than either a ⅔, or full ration: a result which indicates a similar soil condition to that found in the Kingston experiment. A litmus paper test of the soil reveals a decided acid reaction.

1893. *Nitrate of soda gave considerably the best crop:* the yield of hard corn from each plot was only about 3 bushels less than that of last season. Dried blood again held the second place, but the yields were from 5 to 9 bushels per plot less than those of last season. Sulfate of ammonia gave the same marked injurious effect from the larger applications. The results for the four years of the experiment are given in the following computation of yields per acre :

SUMMARY HOPE VALLEY EXPERIMENT,
1890-1893, INCLUSIVE.

		Plot Numbers.	TOTAL YIELDS PER ACRE IN 4 YEARS.		
			HARD CORN. Bus.	SOFT CORN. Bus.	STOVER. Pounds.
Nitrate of Soda Group,	-	7	126.39	14.72	8964
		8	176.50	13.69	11632
		9	162.15	13.95	11147
	TOTALS,	.....	465.04	42.36	31743
Sulfate of Ammonia Group,	-	10	115.30	15.07	9275
		11	129.86	16.91	9696
		12	106.49	16.19	8751
	TOTALS,	.....	351.65	48.17	27722
Dried Blood Group,	- -	13	123.85	13.05	8833
		14	137.22	15.00	10820
		15	143.69	15.10	10502
	TOTALS,	.....	404.76	43.15	30155

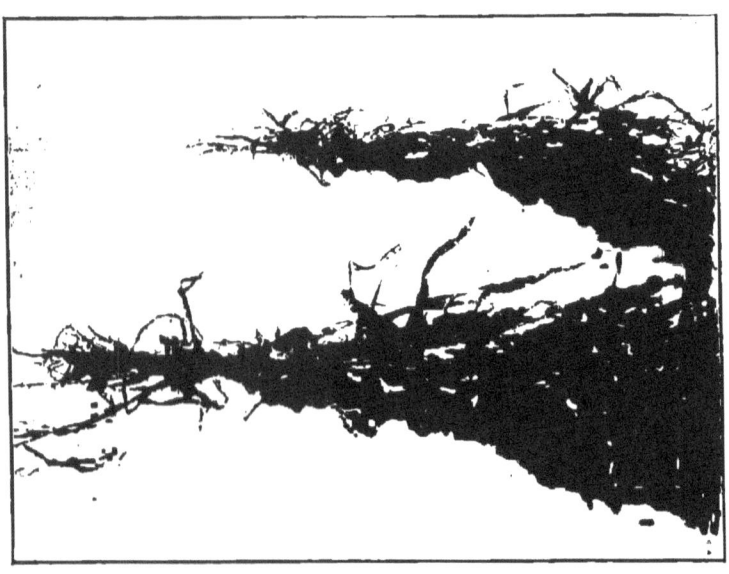

Lime.   No lime.
Sulfate of Ammonia.

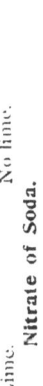

Lime.   No lime.
Nitrate of Soda.

If we compare the figures in the above table of total yields for the four years, we find that the *nitrate of soda group*, as in the preceding experiments, *ranks first*, dried blood second and sulfate of ammonia third. Almost half, 159.64 bushels, of the total yield of hard corn in the sulfate of ammonia group was, however, produced in the first year of the experiment. Both dried blood and sulfate of ammonia gave greater relative yields in this experiment than in either of the preceding, and the total yield produced by each of the three groups was also greater, as may readily be seen by the following summary of totals :

SUMMARY OF TOTAL YIELDS IN FOUR YEARS.

		HARD CORN. Bus.	SOFT CORN. Bus.	STOVER. Pounds.
Nitrate of Soda Group...	Kingston......	420.59	42.01	31918
	Abbott Run ...	441.46	21.10	27840
	Hope Valley...	465.04	42.36	31743
Sulfate of Ammonia Group......	Kingston......	206.43	38.15	17668
	Abbott Run ...	242.35	48.52	21385
	Hope Valley...	351.65	48.17	27722
Dried Blood Group.. ...	Kingston......	339.37	51.22	28451
	Abbott Run ...	266.68	28.09	26235
	Hope Valley...	404.76	43.15	30155

The *superiority of nitrate of soda* as a source of nitrogen for the Indian corn crop is quite evident from the above figures.

These three experiments were the only ones conducted through *four* years, and the *single element* tests showed that phosphoric acid was much needed in every instance, more so than potash ; and nitrogen in any form would not produce a maximum effect without the "mixed minerals" This was quite to be expected, considering that two of these experiment fields were parts of old cow pastures, and the other a field much worn by long and exhaustive cropping. All three were very light sandy-loam soils.

Beginning in 1890, three other experiments were conducted in other sections of the state for a period of three years, and two, for two years. In each instance the land was laid out, fertilized, and the experiment carried on in accordance with the rules which governed the preceding experiments.

4. WESTERLY, R. I.

FARM OF COURTLAND P. CHAPMAN.

The soil of the field selected for experiment was a rather rich, slightly sandy, loam. In 1884 seaweed and stable manure were used to grow Indian corn ; in 1885 seaweed and "phosphate" were used to grow potatoes. In 1886 it was sown to oats and grass, and until 1890 had been regularly mowed and but lightly top-dressed. This field appeared to be in a higher state of fertility than any other under experiment, and large applications of fertilizers, especially the most expensive element, nitrogen, showed less profit than upon poorer soils. The following table shows the yields per acre.

NOTES AND CONCLUSIONS.

1890. Owing to the natural fertility of the field, the yields from all the plots were much larger than was the case in any of the previous experiments. There was almost no difference in the total product of *hard corn* from the *nitrate of soda* group as compared with the dried blood group. *Nitrate of soda* was, however, a shade superior in yield, and gave some 240 pounds more of stover, and, considering its lower cost, was, therefore, fully entitled to the first place as source of nitrogen. The total yield from the sulfate of ammonia group was 16 bushels of hard corn less than was produced by the *nitrate of soda* group.

1891. There was a large falling off in the yields from all the plots, but the relation between the different groups was about the same as in the previous season. The dried blood group this season slightly exceeded the *nitrate of soda* group in both total yield of hard corn and stover. The yields of stover were very uniform for the three groups, a difference of only 100 pounds existing between the highest and the lowest total yield.

1892. The yields were larger than in '91, but not so large as in '90, and much greater relative difference existed. *Nitrate of soda* was this season *most decidedly superior* to both other forms of nitrogen. The total product from the *nitrate of soda* group was 50.29 bushels of hard corn and 2320 pounds of stover more than was produced by the dried blood group. The sulfate of ammonia group gave this season a better crop of hard corn than the dried blood group, but the latter

	1890			1891			1892		
	Hard Corn. Bus.	Soft Corn. Bus.	Stover. Pounds.	Hard Corn. Bus.	Soft Corn. Bus.	Stover. Pounds.	Hard Corn. Bus.	Soft Corn. Bus.	Stover. Pounds.
Nitrate of Soda Group.									
Plot 7, ¼ ration..........	86.86	2.28	1720	33.57	9.28	2600	56.00	1.14	2800
" 8, ½ "	83.43	2.28	4240	35.00	9.28	2700	64.00	2.28	4960
" 9, Full "	64.00	2.28	3440	37.85	10.71	2950	74.28	3.42	5840
Sulfate of Ammonia Group.									
Plot 10, ¼ ration.........	72.00	.28	3440	31.42	8.57	2800	52.57	2.08	3120
" 11, ½ "	65.43	3.42	3120	35.71	6.42	2750	62.85	2.28	3120
" 12, Full "	78.86	2.28	4240	24.28	9.28	2650	64.00	1.14	4000
Dried Blood Group.									
Plot 13, ¼ ration.........	65.43	2.28	3040	35.71	7.85	2500	34.28	4.57	3040
" 14, ½ "	81.14	2.28	4560	34.28	12.14	2800	53.71	2.28	3760
" 15, Full "	85.71	4.57	4560	38.57	10.00	3000	56.71	3.42	4480

produced over half a ton per acre more stover than the former. The total yields for the three years are as follows :

SUMMARY WESTERLY EXPERIMENT, 1890-1892, INCLUSIVE.

		Plot Num-bers.	TOTAL YIELDS PER ACRE IN 3 YEARS.		
			HARD CORN. Bus.	SOFT CORN. Bus.	STOVER. Pounds.
Nitrate of Soda Group	-	7	176.43	12.70	10120
		8	182.43	13.84	11900
		9	176.13	16.41	12230
	TOTALS,	......	534.99	42.95	34250
Sulfate of Ammonia Group,	-	10	155.99	10.93	9360
		11	165.99	12.12	8990
		12	167.14	12.70	10890
	TOTALS,	......	489.12	35.75	29240
Dried Blood Group,	-	13	137.42	14.70	8580
		14	169.13	16.70	11120
		15	175.28	17.99	12640
	TOTALS,	......	481.83	49.39	32340

The above figures show that the *nitrate of soda* group produced the greatest total yield of hard corn and also of stover in the crops of three years. Sulfate of ammonia slightly exceeded dried blood in the total yield of hard corn, but the latter had a considerable excess of soft corn and stover. This soil was a stronger and much richer one than that of any one of the preceding experiments. It contained very much more humus, and doubtless a larger supply of available mineral plant food. While much larger yields were secured than from the experiments upon rather poor and "hungry" sandy soils, the application of nitrogen in any form in large amounts was more profitable in dollars and cents upon the latter. In this experiment the greatest profit came from the use of the $\frac{1}{3}$ ration of nitrogen.

5. NOOSE NECK, R. I.

FARM OF J. B. VAUGHN.

The field in which this experiment was located had not been

plowed or fertilized since 1884, when fodder corn had been planted in drills, with manure. The soil was a poor sandy loam with little or no sod, and when the plots were staked out, little besides bluets (*Houstonia caerulea*) and bird foot violet (*viola pedeta*) was growing upon it. The crops produced upon the three groups of nitrogen plots, calculated to yields per acre, were as follows:

	1890			1891			1892		
	HARD CORN. Bus.	SOFT CORN. Bus.	STOVER. Pounds.	HARD CORN. Bus.	SOFT CORN. Bus.	STOVER. Pounds.	HARD CORN. Bus.	SOFT CORN. Bus.	STOVER. Pounds.
Nitrate of Soda Group.									
Plot 7, ½ ration.........	32.86	7.14	2000	32.50	1.43	1850	14.85	6.28	3010
" 8, ¾ "	39.28	3.57	2400	41.43	.71	1800	26.07	5.35	2820
" 9, Full "	50.00	4.28	2200	38.93	1.43	1675	35.71	4.28	3160
Sulfate of Ammonia Group.									
Plot 10, ½ ration.......	35.71	2.86	2300	26.07	.36	1650	13.78	3.14	2965
" 11, ¾ "	44.28	3.57	2900	40.35	.36	1775	16.78	4.78	2550
" 12, Full "	44.28	2.86	2000	41.78	1.43	2300	21.00	4.42	2920
Dried Blood Group.									
Plot 13, ½ ration.......	38.57	2.14	1500	38.21	.71	1850	4.64	2.28	2575
" 14, ¾ "	36.43	4.28	2300	33.93	.71	1825	8.85	3.42	2720
" 15, Full "	36.43	3.57	2100	41.07	1.07	2000	21.50	3.42	2955

NOTES AND CONCLUSIONS.

1890. The largest yields were upon those plots where nitrogen was added to the "mixed minerals." Nitrogen seemed to be the element most lacking, although potash and phosphoric acid were also deficient. "So far as the eye could detect there was little difference between the the *nitrate* of *soda* and the sulfate of ammonia groups, other than that the latter plots were not so mature as the former." "Nitrogen in the form of *nitrate of soda* and sulfate of ammonia, gave *better returns* than in the form of dried blood, and its application, even in considerable quantities, in the two former cases was accompanied by profit, and in the latter case by loss."

"The corn upon the plots supplied with nitrogen in the form of sulfate of ammonia, was *later in maturing* than where nitrogen in the form of *nitrate of soda* was used."

"Potash and phosphoric acid applied alone proved unprofitable, which was not the case when combined with nitrogen in the most available form."

1891. Sulfate of ammonia, which gave a trifle the largest crop last year, was third in order this season, and dried blood was first, but exceeded *nitrate of soda* by only 0.35 of a bushel of hard corn and 350 pounds of stover.

"Since the field was especially lacking in phosphoric acid, the good showing for the blood may, probably, to some extent be due to the amount of phosphoric acid which it contained." (The dried blood contained 3.21 per cent. of phosphoric acid, while that obtained in 1892 for these experiments contained only 0.42 of a per cent.)

1892. This third season the *nitrate* of *soda* group produced *yields much greater* than were produced by either of the other groups A lack of seasonable rains, from which the crop suffered, may in part account for the reduced yields from the sulfate of ammonia and dried blood groups; the soil being too dry for nitrification to go on with sufficient rapidity to furnish the necessary nitrates for plant growth.

"*Nitrate of soda gave by far the best results*, while sulfate of ammonia and dried blood did not produce yields commensurate with their cost.

Following is the table of total yields for three years :

SUMMARY NOOSE NECK EXPERIMENT,

1890-1892, INCLUSIVE.

	Plot Numbers.	TOTAL YIELDS PER ACRE IN 3 YEARS.		
		HARD CORN. Bus.	SOFT CORN. Bus.	STOVER. Pounds.
Nitrate of Soda Group, -	7	80.21	9.85	6860
	8	106.78	9.57	7020
	9	124.64	9.99	8335
TOTALS,	......	**311.63**	**29.31**	**22215**
Sulfate of Ammonia Group, -	10	75.56	6.36	6845
	11	101.41	8.71	6925
	12	107.06	8.71	7820
TOTALS,	......	284.03	23.78	21590
Dried Blood Group, - -	13	71.42	5.13	5725
	14	79.21	8.41	6845
	15	99.00	8.06	7035
TOTALS,	......	249.63	21.60	19605

The total yields for the three years from the _nitrate of soda group,_
exceeded the yields in either of the other groups, in hard corn, soft corn,
and stover. Sulfate of ammonia produced the next best yield, as the
total produced by the dried blood group was cut down considerably by
the small yield in 1892.

6, JAMESTOWN, R. I.

FARM OF T. A. H. TEFFT.

This experiment was located on the north end of the island of
Conanicut. The soil was a black loam. The field had been in grass
for forty years, and had received no top dressing in any form for seven
or eight years, except across one corner of some of the single element plots. The land was plowed 4½ inches deep. The ends of some
of the plots were too low and wet for the corn crop, but, in harvesting,
a given section of the whole plot, representing a normal yield, was
weighed, and the weights for the whole plot calculated from this. In

1891 a portion of a field located upon higher ground, and better adapted to the corn crop, was selected for experiment. The soil was a light sand, with gravelly subsoil. The last application of manure was about twelve years ago, since which time it has grown two crops of corn, one each of oats and rye, and several crops of grass. The soil was very badly "run down," and only occasional tufts of grass covered the surface. The following table gives the yields upon the plots of the two fields, calculated to yields per acre :

	1890 (1st Field.)			1891 (2d Field.)		
	HARD CORN. Bus.	SOFT CORN. Bus.	STOVER. Pounds.	HARD CORN. Bus.	SOFT CORN. Bus.	STOVER. Pounds.
Nitrate of Soda Group.						
Plot 7, ¼ ration............	65.71	12.86	3800	41.42	11.43	3000
" 8, ⅜ "	70.00	10.00	4300	50.00	6.78	3600
" 9, Full "	72.86	11.43	4600	51.42	7.85	3400
Sulfate of Ammonia Group.						
Plot 10, ¼ ration............	57.14	17.14	3400	34.28	7.14	2850
" 11, ⅜ "	60.00	15.71	3700	43.57	5.71	3600
" 12, Full "	65.71	17.14	4000	26.43	7.14	2900
Dried Blood Group.						
Plot 13, ¼ ration............	37.14	12.86	2800	22.14	5.71	2400
" 14, ⅜ "	38.57	11.43	2000	24.28	8.57	2800
" 15, Full "	37.14	15.71	2900	15.71	7.14	2100

NOTES AND CONCLUSIONS.

1890. The plots comprising the *nitrate* of *Soda* group gave considerably *the best yields*, and a profitable increase over the yield from "mixed minerals" without nitrogen. The plots in the sulfate of ammonia group ranked second in yield, but the corn was later in maturing, and the yield of soft corn was large. The dried blood, for some reason, seemed to be of no advantage, as the yield from the mixed mineral plots on either side of this group, without addition of nitrogen, gave larger yields.

1891. The soil of this field was very poor sandy loam, quite unlike that used the previous season. The yields were not so large as from the other field, but again *nitrate of soda gave by far the best results*, sulfate of ammonia ranked second, and dried blood gave the smallest yields. As this experiment was not consecutive upon the same field, we omit a summary of the yields for two years. The superior yields from the use of *nitrate* of *soda* are very evident in both instances, and its lower cost adds to the economy of its use.

An experiment was conducted for three years upon the farm of Copwell and Tillinghast, at Summit, and one for two years upon the farm of H. Hartwell Jencks, Lime Rock, but as considerable inequality in the natural fertility of the different plots was apparent in the results, we will not take space for the details. An experiment was conducted for one season in three other localities in the state, but as the results are all summarized in the "Conclusions" by Dr. Wheeler in 1890, and later by Mr. Lowar, we quote from their reports in relation to the use of materials for the supply of nitrogen.

1890. "Nitrogen proved most profitable upon soils with little sod and humus, *i. e.*, light sandy, or gravelly, loams. Taking all the experiments into consideration, nitrogen in the form of *nitrate* of *soda was more certain to give fair returns than in either of the other forms. Its lesser cost is, also, an additional argument in its favor.*"

"The sulfate of ammonia gave, in one or two instances, better returns than *nitrate of soda*, though in two cases, at least, the period of growth was prolonged by its use which may, perhaps, have been due to delayed nitrification. In one instance[1], the sulfate nitrogen appears not only not to have been available to the plant, but to have had a decidedly injurious effect, for it more than neutralized the otherwise good effect of the potash and phosphoric acid with which it was applied. The greater the application of the sulfate, the more disastrous were the results."

"On the whole, nitrogen in the form of dried blood proved inferior to both the other forms."

1891. "While in four cases, in 1890, potash appeared the most deficient, it has in no case, upon a second trial been found so much lacking as phosphoric acid."

"Of the three forms of nitrogen, *nitrate of soda has, upon the whole, proved the most profitable*, and sulfate of ammonia the least."

"In most of the plots where dried blood was applied, the corn

---

[1] Used upon a soil having a decided acid re-action.

ripened earlier, and showed, when compared with the *nitrate of soda*
and sulphate of ammonia plots, a greater relative yield than in 1890.
This gain may be due to the fact that the dried blood contained, in
addition to the organic nitrogen, a small amount of phosphoric acid,
and this amount was unusually great in the blood used in 1891. The
phosphoric acid may have increased the yield. Another cause for the
increase might be, since nitrification of dried blood is somewhat slow,
that, in all probability, some of the nitrogen applied on these plots in
1890 was unused until 1891."

1892. " Phosphoric acid has in every case proved itself the most
deficient, followed by nitrogen. "

In the special nitrogen tests, *nitrate of soda takes first place in all but
one instance, where it holds second place.* Sulfate of ammonia holds first
place once, second place twice and third place three times. Dried
blood holds second and third places three times each.

" The ill effects of sulfate of ammonia were wholly prevented by
the application of air-slaked lime. "

1893. The three experiments continued through four years,
showed by *considerably increased crops the superior effect of nitrate of soda*
as a source of nitrogen. If we represent the total product from the
nitrate of soda groups, in the three experiments, for the whole time, by
100 in the case of the hard corn, soft corn and stover, then the products
in the other two groups would be represented as follows : The relative
cost of the fertilizers for the three groups, calculated on the same basis,
is also included in the table.

	Hard corn.	Soft Corn.	Stover.	Cost.
Nitrate of Soda group,	100.0	100.0	100.0	100.0
Sulfate of Ammonia group,	60.3	127.8	72.9	105.0
Dried Blood group,	76.1	116.1	92.7	107.4

These figures show plainly the *proportional gains in hard corn and
stover made by the nitrate of soda group,* in these three experiments, considered as a unit, and also the increased proportional cost of the
fertilizers for the dried blood and sulfate of ammonia groups, as compared with that of the *nitrate of soda* group. In the *case of the soft corn
the nitrate of soda gave the smallest yield,* dried blood yielding about one-
sixth more, and sulfate of ammonia fully one quarter more. This
result in the totals of these experiments for a term of years, is in accord
with observations in the case of individual experiments already noticed,
when the corn upon the dried blood and sulfate of ammonia plots,

particularly the latter, required a considerably longer time to mature than was required for that upon the *nitrate of soda* plots. This point in favor of the use of *nitrate of soda* has an important bearing upon the use of fertilizers in northern latitudes.

COWPEA.
Plot Nos. 29. Limed.   27. Unlimed.   25. Limed.   23. Unlimed.
Nitrate of Soda.   **Sulfate of Ammonia.**
All manured alike with Potash and Phosphoric Acid.

EXPERIMENTS WITH A VARIETY OF CROPS.[1]

The marked ill effect of increased applications of sulfate of ammonia to the corn crop in the "Twentieth-acre Cooperative Experiment," on the grounds of the Experiment Station at Kingston, R. I., and the fact that applications of air-slaked lime corrected the ill effects,

CANTALOUPE.
Plot Nos. 29. Limed.   27. Unlimed.   25. Limed.   23. Unlimed.
Nitrate of Soda.   **Sulfate of Ammonia.**
All manured alike with Potash and Phosphoric Acid.

as already stated, led to the institution of an experiment upon four of the permanent plots, located a short distance to the south, upon the same level sandy loam plain land. These plots are separated from each other by unmanured spaces of three feet, and are so laid out that

[1] Compiled from the Annual Reports of the Rhode Island Agricultural Experiment Station, from 1893 to 1897, inclusive. The experiment was in charge of Dr. H. J. Wheeler, chemist, assisted by the Agricultural Division.

a border of three feet upon each side, and six feet across each end, is fertilized at the same rate and cultivated in the same way as the real plot which lies within. This permits the discarding from the experiment the *outside rows*, which necessarily obtain more air, light and room than interior ones, and, thus, only results from interior rows, which approximate field conditions, are used for comparative work. The interior plots are 181½ feet long and 24 feet wide, making an area of $\frac{1}{10}$ of an acre. In 1891 a crop of beans, and in 1892 a crop of Indian corn had been grown without manures upon these plots, for the purpose of ascertaining if they were suitable for comparative work. As they proved very uniform in quality, were level, parallel and adjacent to each other, they were well adapted to the work proposed, viz., the use of nitric and ammoniacal forms of nitrogen, with and with-

SOJA BEAN.

Plot Nos. 29. Limed.   27. Unlimed.   25. Limed.   23. Unlimed.
Nitrate of Soda.   **Sulfate of Ammonia.**
All manured alike with Potash and Phosphoric Acid.

out lime, in the growth of a variety of farm and garden crops. We have thus far studied the effect of *nitrate of soda* upon the corn crop alone. We have now to observe its effect upon a great variety of crops, including grasses, nursery stock and small fruits.

The four plots were manured alike with muriate of potash, at the rate of 200 pounds per acre, and dissolved bone-black at the rate of 600 pounds per acre. Plots 23 and 25, toward the west, received an additional dressing of 360 pounds per acre of sulfate of ammonia, and the two toward the east, 27 and 29, a dressing of *nitrate of soda* at the rate of 465 pounds per acre, or at such a rate that the *amount of nitrogen applied upon each plot was exactly the same.* One of the sulfate of ammonia plots, No. 25, and one of the nitrate of soda plots, No. 29, received, in addition, a dressing of air-slaked lime at the rate of 5400 pounds per acre. The lime was applied by itself and thoroughly harrowed in. The other fertilizers were carefully applied broadcast, and well worked in by harrowing. Seeds of a large variety of crops were planted in rows three feet apart, running across all four plots. The following table shows the weights of the various crops, obtained from a given and equal length of row on each of the four plots.

MANGEL WURZEL.

Plot Nos. 29. Limed.   27. Unlimed.   25. Limed. 23. Unlimed.
        Nitrate of Soda.   **Sulfate of Ammonia.**
        All manured alike with Potash or Phosphoric Acid.

There are 43 weights given in each column of the above table, representing 37 different crops, and from the *unlimed* plots, 23 and 27, the same amount of nitrogen in *nitrate of soda* upon plot 27 as compared with a like quantity of nitrogen in sulfate of ammonia upon plot 23, *produced a heavier crop in every case.* In 9 instances in the case of the sulfate of ammonia, plot 23, there were no weights to record. The

CABBAGE.

Plot Nos. 29. Limed.   27. Unlimed.   25. Limed. 23. Unlimed.
        Nitrate of Soda.   **Sulfate of Ammonia.**
        All manured alike with Potash and Phosphoric Acid.

total failures included all four varieties of beets, Jerusalem corn, early and late cabbage (trimmed heads), spinach and merchantable potatoes. All the conditions of seed and planting, care of crops and harvesting, were, so far as possible, identical in the case of these four plots. In planting all the small seeds, the seed-sower was run directly across the

TABLE I.

1893	UNLIMED.		LIMED.	
	Plot 23. Sulfate of Amm'nia Lbs.	Plot 27. Nitrate of Soda. Lbs.	Plot 25. Sulfate of Amm'nia Lbs.	Plot 29. Nitrate of Soda. Lbs.
Crimson clover	3.75	19.50	20.75	26.50
White beans (as pulled)	4.12	4.81	5.94	5.25
White podded adzuki beans (soy)	13.62	22.81	22.87	18.00
Cow pea (green)	10.37	12.00	12.31	9.44
Soy bean "	9.38	21.81	7.88	18.00
Blue lupine (as harvested)	12.63	14.44	4.25	5.56
"Granger" pea (pods and vines)	.44	1.88	4.94	2.88
White capped corn (green)	3.06	12.63	13.69	8.75
Dent corn "	2.50	9.25	15.00	9.88
Pop-corn "	3.69	18.63	27.25	30.00
Sweet corn "	2.95	14.13	24.50	29.75
Eclipse table beet (roots and tops)	.25	9.00	42.00	69.25
French sugar beets " "	.00	5.25	60.75	94.75
Long red mangels " "	.00	9.80	61.00	75.50
Golden tankard beets " "	.00	7.25	48.50	68.00
Victoria carrots " "	.00	25.00	42.50	40.50
Mastodon carrots " "	.44	29.00	70.50	50.00
Rutabagas (Swedish turnips) "	13.25	75.75	65.25	115.50
Amber sugar cane (green)	.02	.56	13.19	7.50
Kaffir corn "	.05	2.44	11.63	9.19
Jerusalem corn "	.00	.50	2.75	1.75
Sunflowers (seeds and stalks)	3.25	40.19	54.88	43.80
Kale (green)	16.06	92.56	119.56	139.56
Early cabbage (total crop)	10.50	90.50	97.25	116.50
" " (trimmed heads)	.00	52.75	50.50	57.00
Late cabbage (total crop)[1]	16.75	46.00	120.00	109.00
" " (trimmed heads)	.00	10.00	40.00	68.00
Spinach (green)	.00	.69	9.38	18.38
Early rose potatoes (total crop)	6.25	13.56	13.50	13.94
" " " (large tubers)[2]	.00	2.98	6.16	7.36
Tomatoes (total fruit)	3.07	29.63	25.81	41.62
" (ripe fruit)	1.63	15.69	15.31	10.06
" (unripe fruit)	1.44	13.94	10.50	31.56
" (vines, green)	7.81	16.13	13.81	26.50
Lettuce	.63	.13	7.63	10.13
Oats, straw and grain (as harvested)	4.44	5.56	5.31	7.50
Barley " " "	.50	2.88	3.94	5.31
Rye " " "	1.00	2.13	2.25	2.06
Hungarian (green)	1.81	8.75	10.69	8.31
Golden millet "	1.19	12.63	16.44	14.13
Italian " "	2.50	19.56	21.38	16.75
Panicum crus-galli (green)	12.13	43.06	41.25	58.00
Buckwheat "	43.38	66.19	73.25	97.19

[1] But few of this variety reached maturity.
[2] Tubers 2 oz. or more in weight.

four plots, including the three-foot paths which separated them, thus insuring the same rate of seeding and depth of covering. After the plants were up, lines were stretched and the paths hoed out. The beet seed germinated as well upon plot 23 as upon any one of the others, but the young plants soon stopped growing, turned a sickly

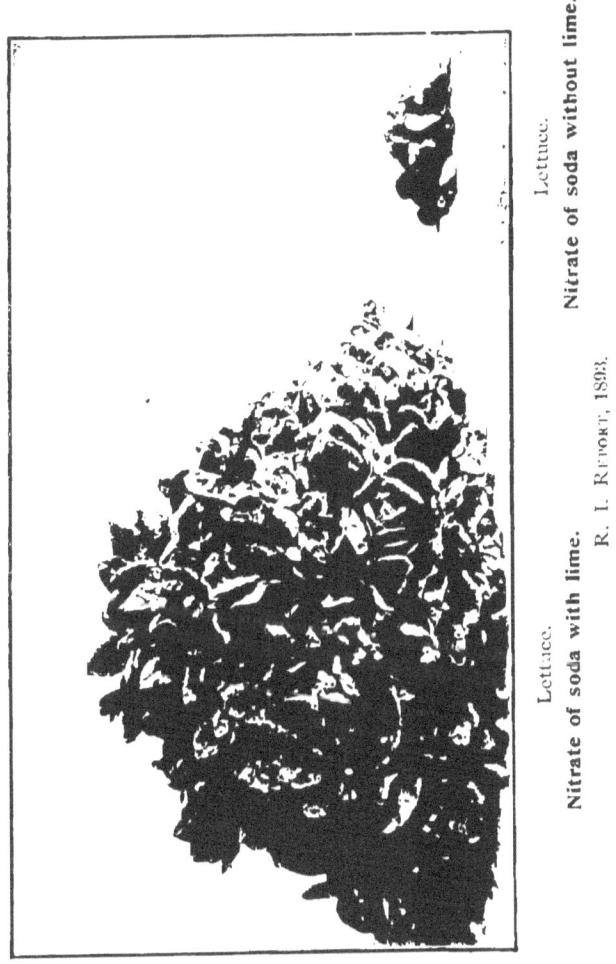

Lettuce.
Nitrate of soda without lime.

R. I. REPORT, 1893.

Lettuce.
Nitrate of soda with lime.

red hue and died. The beets upon plot 27, where *nitrate of soda* was used, made some growth, but not a profitable one, as compared with the crop produced by the same amount of fertilizer in connection with lime on plot 29. Spinach and lettuce are also very susceptible to soil acidity and greatly benefitted by the *use of lime in connection with nitrate of soda upon such soils.*

The reader may say that these are unusual results due to very peculiar soil conditions, but considerable investigation, very many litmus paper soil tests, and a number of experiments in the growing of beets, barley, clover and grass (in which, however, there was no comparison of forms of nitrogen) show that very large areas of land in this and other states are affected by similar conditions to a

SUGAR BEETS

Plot Nos. 29. Limed.   27. Unlimed.   25. Limed.   23. Unlimed.
       Nitrate of Soda.   **Sulfate of Ammonia.**
       All manured alike with Potash and Phosphoric Acid.

greater or less extent. These plots are surrounded by hundreds of acres of land of a similar character, *i.e.*, level, light sandy loam, naturally well drained, but thin soil, more or less exhausted by long continued cropping, so that the above results can by no means be claimed as peculiar to the particular plots used for the experiment.

Turning to the limed plots, 25 and 29, we find that *nitrate of soda gave greater yields in 25 out of the 43 weights.* The application of lime was

TABLE BEETS.

Plot Nos. 29. Limed.   27. Unlimed.   25. Limed.   23. Unlimed.
       Nitrate of Soda.   **Sulfate of Ammonia.**
       All manured alike with Potash and Phosphoric Acid.

quite a heavy one, about two and three fourths tons per acre (5400 lbs.,) and further investigation has shown that some varieties of plants were perhaps injuriously affected by the large application of lime in conjunction with the *nitrate of soda.* This is particularly applicable to the carrot, which should be planted two or three years after liming rather than immediately after.

The experiment was continued upon the same plots, and in 1894, potash, phosphoric acid and nitrogen were applied, at the same rate

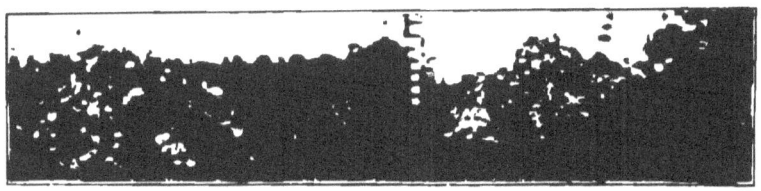

CELERY.

Plot Nos. 29. Limed.   27. Unlimed.   25. Limed.   23. Unlimed.
Nitrate of Soda.   **Sulfate of Ammonia.**
All manured alike with Potash and Phosphoric Acid.

and in the same forms, upon the respective plots as in 1893. An additional application of half a ton per acre of air-slaked lime was applied to plots 25 and 29, which had been limed the previous season.

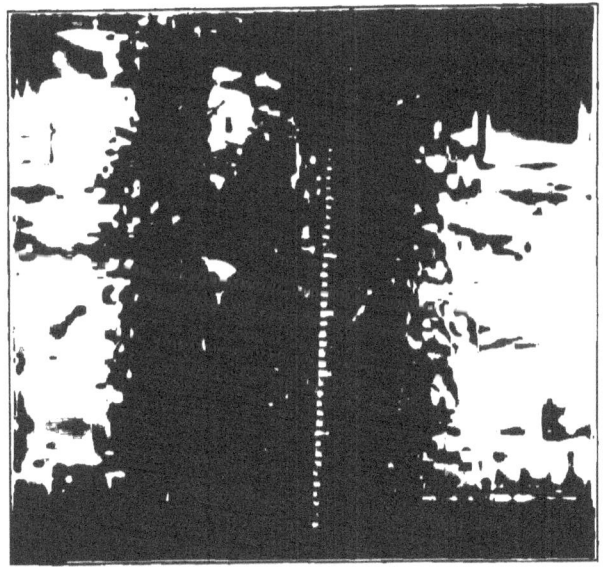

SORGHUM.

Plot Nos. 29. Limed.   27. Unlimed.   25. Limed.   23. Unlimed.
Nitrate of Soda.   **Sulfate of Ammonia.**
All manured alike with Potash and Phosphoric Acid.

This was done because the soil of these plots was found to be still slightly acid. As before, the different crops were planted, or set in rows, generally three feet apart, directly across the plots, but in the case

TABLE II.

1894	Plot 23. Sulfate of Amm'nia. Lbs.	Plot 27. Nitrate of Soda. Lbs.	Plot 25. Sulfate of Amm nia. Lbs.	Plot 29. Nitrate of Soda. Lbs.
	UNLIMED.		LIMED.	
Spinach	0.0	0.1	2.2	6.1
Gumbo	0.0	2.1	20.0	23.8
Sugar beet	0.0	3.0	25.0	33.0
Lettuce	0.0	0·6	3.1	6.0
Salsify (whole plant)	0.0	2.5	24.5	27.0
Celery	0.8	4.3	23.0	40.5
Onion (red)	0.0	2.0	8.0	18.0
" (yellow)	0.0	1.6	5.5	13.0
Globe Mangel-wurzel	0.0	5.3	23.8	43.5
Long " " (roots and tops)	0.0	27.3	51.1	135.0
Table beets	0.0	11.5	40.0	61.5
Muskmelon (fruit)	0.0	7.1	29.9	33.4
Late cabbage (trimmed heads)	0.0	7.0	34.6	71.0
Tobacco	1.8	9.5	38.3	43.0
Egg-plant (fruit)	2.3	4.0	1.8	15.1
Cauliflower (heads)	0.0	1.8	1.8	3.5
Cucumber (fruit)	0.7	28.9	36.1	87.3
Sorghum	0.0	23.6	58.4	70.5
Martynia (whole plant)	1.0	17.8	22.5	50.6
Pepper (fruit)	0.1	2.3	4.5	6.3
Peanut	3.8	5.5	3.3	3.9
Barley (air dried)	0.1	1.8	3.6	3.7
Rape	0.0	58.0	97.8	114.4
Red clover (air dried)	0.2	4.1	9.5	7.0
Potato, Beauty of Hebron (tubers)	5.2	16.5	23.4	....
Potato, Early Rose (tubers)	1.3	9.3	8.3	9.8
Garden peas	0.1	8.0	13.7	14.2
Kohl Rabi	0.5	5.9	9.3	9.4
Brussels sprouts	6.3	64.6	95.3	101.4
Golden wax bean (beans and pods, ripe)	0.0	2.4	3.3	3.8
Buckwheat (air dried)	0.8	3.8	5.5	5.8
Rutabaga, or Swedish turnip	1.5	45.5	59.8	66.5
Tomato (fruit)	13.9	157.8	170.9	215.2
Sunflower	0.8	59.3	69.3	84.0
Spring wheat (air dried)	0.1	0.5	0.8	0.7
Radish, long scarlet	0.6	4.6	1.8	6.3
Turnip, strop leaf	2.5	38.0	35.5	44.0
Early Cabbage (trimmed heads)	2.0	55.3	71.3	63.1
Danvers carrot	0.6	27.1	24.0	19.4
White "	0.0	16.4	13.4	19.4
Improved long orange carrot	0.0	12.1	9.8	9.0
Kale	9.4	64.8	95.0	94.4
Sweet corn	0 0	48.3	62.1	53.5
Oats (air dried)	0.7	3.2	4.6	3.5

of beets, spinach, lettuce, and a few other crops, the young plants upon plot 23 practically all died before the time when the second or third leaves should have appeared. On the preceding page we give a condensed table of the results obtained in 1894:

TABLE II, CONTINUED.

1894	UNLIMED.		LIMED.	
	Plot 23. Sulfate of Amm'nia. Lbs.	Plot 27. Nitrate of Soda. Lbs.	Plot 25. Sulfate of Amm'nia. Lbs.	Plot 29. Nitrate of Soda. Lbs.
Dandelion.........	0.0	16.6	16.8	17.9
Soy bean.........................	4.8	44.0	62.0	46.5
Spring rye (air dried)..................	1.5	3.9	3.9	4.0
Cowpea	10.4	38.5	33.0	36.0
German millet (air dried)..............	0.6	7.0	5.3	6.3
Common white bean (whole plant)......	1.0	6.8	6.3	6.0
Radish, French breakfast	0.4	3.8	1.6	3.3
Golden millet (air dried)...............	0.5	9.6	8.8	8.4
Watermelon (fruit)..................	85.5	249.6	141.7	160.4
R. I. capped corn (ears and stover)......	0.0	28.3	27.0	17.8
Pumpkin (fruit).......	0.0	87.2	31.5	48.5
Blue Lupine (air dried)................	2.9	6.0	2.9	1.4
Sorrel (common weed).................	84.5	76.0	7.0	27.5

DANDELION.
Plot Nos. 29. Limed. 27. Unlimed. 25. Limed. 23. Unlimed.
Nitrate of Soda.   **Sulfate of Ammonia.**
All manured alike with Potash and Phosphoric Acid.

In this trial we have a wide variety of field and garden crops, and one weed, sorrel, was included because of the common impression that it thrives best upon an acid soil. In the 57 records made in the above table, comparing the unlimed plots, 23 and 27, we find that this season, as well as last, *nitrate of soda has produced a greater yield in every instance*

ALFALFA.

Plot Nos. 29. Limed.　27. Unlimed.　25. Limed.　23. Unlimed.

Nitrate of Soda.　　　　　　**Sulfate of Ammonia.**

All manured alike with Potash and Phosphoric Acid.

save one, sorrel, where sulfate of ammonia gave the larger crop. In 22 instances there was no crop whatever from the sulfate of ammonia plot, while in not a single instance did *nitrate of soda* make a complete failure. On the contrary, *nitrate of soda without lime*, in twelve instances, not counting sorrel, produced a larger crop than when lime was added.

GERMAN MILLET.

Plot Nos. 29. Limed.　　27. Unlimed.　25. Limed.　23. Unlimed.

Nitrate of Soda.　　　　　　**Sulfate of Ammonia.**

All manured alike with Potash and Phosphoric Acid.

Comparing the yields from the *limed* plots, 25 and 29, we find that *the crops produced by nitrate of soda have exceeded* those produced by sulfate of ammonia in *44 cases out of the 57 recorded, and in the 13 exceptions we notice that in 6 instances nitrate of soda without lime, plot 27, has given larger yields than sulfate of ammonia with lime, plot 25.* We therefore find *that the yields from nitrate of soda, with or without the addition of lime, have exceeded those from sulfate of ammonia plus lime, in 50 out of 57 trials, embracing a great variety of field and garden crops.*

In 1895, 12 varieties of grasses were sown across the plots, and a number of vegetables, cereals and miscellaneous crops were again planted. Some modifications of the previous manuring were made, as

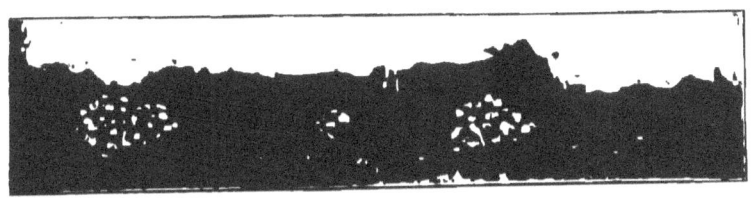

YELLOW ONIONS.

Plot Nos. 29. Limed.   27. Unlimed.   25. Limed.   23. Unlimed.

Nitrate of Soda.   **Sulfate of Ammonia.**

All manured alike with Potash and Phosphoric Acid.

follows: owing to the known deficiency of phosphoric acid in this soil, the application of dissolved bone-black was increased from 600 to 800 pounds per acre: the amount of muriate of potash was also increased from 180 to 350 pounds per acre: the amount of *nitrate of soda* remained the same as in 1894, and a like quantity of nitrogen, in the form of sulfate of ammonia, was applied, each upon its respective plot. No further application of air-slaked lime was made, but sulfate of magnesia

KOHL-RABI.

Plot Nos. 29. Limed.   27. Unlimed.   25. Limed.   23. Unlimed.

Nitrate of Soda.   **Sulfate of Ammonia.**

All manured alike with Potash and Phosphoric Acid.

at the rate of 200 pounds per acre, was applied to all the plots. "This was done for the reason that previously better results had been obtained from the limed plot which received *nitrate of soda* than from the other limed plot which received sulfate of ammonia, differences which might have, in part, been attributed to the liberation of magnesia by the soda."

The months of June and July proved to be very wet as compared with the same months in 1894, when only 1.85 inches of rain fell. During

those two months in 1895, 9.19 inches of rain fell.   It has been observed
that in very wet seasons sulfate of ammonia generally produces better
results than in dry seasons.   This may be due, to some extent, to more
rapid nitrification because of the more abundant moisture, and no
doubt, also, when used upon acid soils, to the fact that the larger
amount of rain falling dilutes the soil moisture and weakens the acid

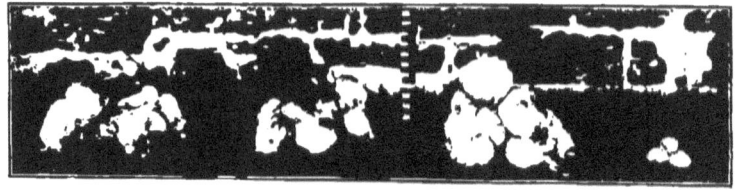

EARLY CABBAGE.

Plot Nos. 29.   Limed.   27. Unlimed.   25. Limed.   23. Unlimed.
               Nitrate of Soda.   **Sulfate of Ammonia.**
        All manured alike with Potash and Phosphoric Acid.

reaction, so that the soil acidity is less injurious to plants.   On the
other hand, such excessive rain falls, coming just after *nitrate of soda* has
been applied, and before the crop has had opportunity to take it up, is
liable to carry some portion of the nitrogen down below the reach of
the plant roots.   It will be seen by the following table of weights of
field and garden plots, that the yields from sulfate of ammonia compare more favorably with those from *nitrate of soda* than heretofore.

WATERMELONS.

Plot Nos. 29. Limed.   27. Unlimed.   25. Limed.   23. Unlimed.
           Nitrate of Soda.   **Sulfate of Ammonia.**
        All manured alike with Potash and Phosphoric Acid.

There are 24 weights given in the table, and only five absolute
failures from plot 23, sulfate of ammonia without lime.   The crops
which absolutely failed were alfalfa, onions, pumpkins, muskmelons and
dandelions, but barley, wheat, celery, mangel-wurzel and table beets,
carrots and cabbages failed to produce more than a fraction of a pound
each.   This plot, however, produced the heaviest yield of watermelons,

in marked contrast to the utter failure of the muskmelons. The yield of oats and rye exceeded that produced upon plot 27, with *nitrate of soda*, by less than a pound each. Therefore, in spite of the better crops produced by the sulfate of ammonia on plot 23, the yields from *nitrate of soda* on plot 27 *were greater in the case of 21 out of 24 crops.* Comparing the yields upon the limed plots, we find that *nitrate of soda* gave the larger yield with 10 crops and sulfate of ammonia with 14, but two of the 14, field corn and serradella, only exceeded the yield from *nitrate of soda* by the fraction of a pound.

TABLE III.

1895	UNLIMED.		LIMED.	
	Plot 23. Sulfate of Amm'nia. Lbs.	Plot 27. Nitrate of Soda. Lbs.	Plot 25. Sulfate of Amm'nia Lbs.	Plot 29. Nitrate of Soda. Lbs.
Barley (avg. of 2 rows)................	0.18	4.35	16.88	15.58
Wheat '' ''	0.38	2.63	6.90	5.03
Oats '' ''	8.48	8.15	10.18	8.75
Rye '' ''	2.78	2.75	3.23	2.05
Sweet corn (ears and stover)....	4.40	25.00	59.80	37.25
Field corn '' ''	2.15	20.90	22.35	22.25
Pop-corn .'' ''	5.75	44.56	42.30	45.98
Panicum crus-galli (millet)............	11.45	19.00	17.20	15.60
Alfalfa (1st and 2nd crop).............	0.00	5.60	16.75	10.60
Sorrel...........................	108.25	124.60	108.60	102.50
Serradella.......................	39.05	56.55	39.65	39.05
Blue lupine......................	30.50	44.00	29.25	25.75
Celery..........................	0.05	0.50	10.55	13.80
Onions (Barletta)	0.00	2.50	9.70	19.70
Pumpkins........................	0.00	25.00	48.60	134.05
Beets, mangel-wurzel................	0.10	24.10	90.65	119.25
Muskmelon	0.00	26.40	47.90	64.60
Carrots.........................	0.15	43.00	83.85	84.45
Table beets......................	0.20	54.10	105.70	99.45
Cabbage (trimmed heads).............	0.60	57.10	70.40	97.15
Kohl-rabi........................	1.80	33.50	57.50	53.55
Dandelion........................	0.00	13.55	20.62	23.58
Flat turnip	28.50	80.00	124.00	107.30
Watermelon......................	136.00	104.75	20.60	57.10

GRASSES.

The grasses were sown in narrow beds across the four plots, the varieties being separated by a cultivated path. As the seed was sown in the spring of 1895, a full crop could hardly be expected that season but all were cut, and the experiment continued for two more seasons. For convenience and brevity we combine the yields for the three years

TIMOTHY.
Plot Nos. 29. Limed.   27. Unlimed.   25. Limed.   23. Unlimed.
Nitrate of Soda.   **Sulfate of Ammonia.**
All manured alike with Potash and Phosphoric Acid.

in one table. Each variety was cut when in full bloom, or as soon thereafter as possible. The weights for timothy in 1895 were unfortunately lost. The weights given are of undried material.

SWEET CORN (MAIZE).
Plot No. 29. Limed. 27. Unlimed.   25. Limed.   23. Unlimed.
Nitrate of Soda.   **Sulfate of Ammonia.**
All manured alike with Potash and Phosphoric Acid.

The figures in the following table do not represent pure cultures of the several varieties, for, while as good seed as could be had was used, there was some intermixture of other grasses, or plants, in every case.

TABLE IV.

VARIETIES OF GRASSES.	Year.	UNLIMED.		LIMED.	
		Plot 23. Sulfate of Amm'nia Lbs.	Plot 27. Nitrate of Soda. Lbs.	Plot 25. Sulfate of Amm'nia Lbs.	Plot 29. Nitrate of Soda. Lbs.
Awnless Brome Grass, (*Bromus inermis*).	1895	11.25	17.75	27.00	27.50
	1896	10.13	13.15	19.05	15.90
	1897	9.30	9.00	9.50	9.50
TOTALS,		30.68	39.90	55.55	52.90
Meadow Fox-tail, (*Alopecurus pratensis*).	1895	21.75	36.25	41.00	47.00
	1896	26.70	27.70	25.30	24.60
	1897	14.30	12.00	11.50	15.80
TOTALS,		62.75	75.95	77.80	87.40
Tall Fescue, (*Festuca elatior*).	1895	20.25	36.00	42.50	44.50
	1896	24.45	22.40	34.10	33.65
	1897	16.30	14.30	22.80	25.00
TOTALS,		61.00	72.90	99.40	103.15
Kentucky Blue Grass, (*Poa pratensis.*)	1895	1.00	11.00	16.00	13.25
	1896	14.45	14.10	16.50	17.00
	1897	2.30	4.30	3.30	7.00
TOTALS,		17.75	29.40	35.80	37.25
Red Top, (*Agrostis vulgaris*).	1895	26.00	24.00	28.00	28.00
	1896	32.25	27.45	29.65	25.75
	1897	17.00	12.50	14.00	17.50
TOTALS,		72.25	63.95	71.65	71.25
Orchard Grass, (*Dactylis glomerata*).	1895	25.75	40.50	42.00	47.00
	1896	24.40	25.30	29.30	34.55
	1897	10.80	12.40	15.90	15.30
TOTALS,		60.95	78.20	87.20	96.85
Meadow Oat Grass, (*Avena elatior.*)	1895	30.75	35.25	34.75	38.25
	1896	20.50	24.30	24.15	28.10
	1897	13.50	12.50	11.50	16.80
TOTALS,		64.75	72.05	70.40	83.15
Soft Grass, (*Holcus lanatus*).	1895	72.25	68.75	75.25	69.75
	1896	19.15	20.92	26.20	24.50
	1897	11.80	7.30	11.00	17.00
TOTALS,		103.20	96.97	112.45	111.25
Rhode Island Bent, (*Agrostis canina*).	1895	23.00	21.00	25.27	20.75
	1896	29.50	19.30	25.35	22.70
	1897	15.00	13.30	10.50	18.50
TOTALS,		67.50	53.60	61.12	61.95
Sweet Vernal, (*Anthoxanthum od. puelli*).	1895	5.75	9.00	9.25	8.00
	1897	3.70	7.70	6.10	9.20
TOTALS,		9.45	16.70	15.35	17.20
Sheep's Fescue, (*Festuca ovina*).	1895	3.75	1.25	2.50	1.25
	1896	11.50	7.55	13.90	11.40
	1897	8.30	5.30	8.50	12.50
TOTALS,		23.55	14.10	24.90	25.15
Timothy, (*Phleum pratense*).	1896	21 10	25.30	31.05	30.80
	1897	14.10	20.40	23.80	23.70
TOTALS,		35.20	45.70	54.85	54.50

Upon plot 23, in the case of Kentucky blue grass, orchard grass, timothy, and some others, the soil conditions appeared to be unfavorable to their growth, and they only persisted in a feeble way, or gave place to coarser plants. In harvesting it was impossible to separate each variety

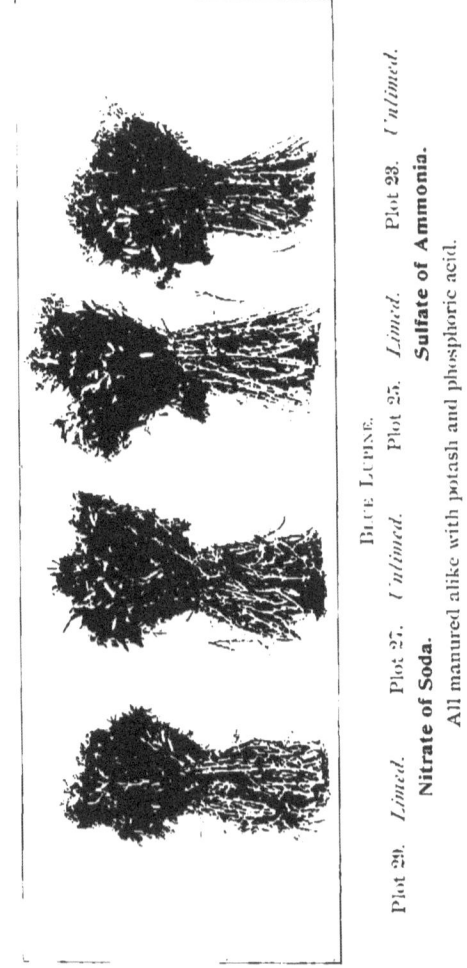

Plot 29. *Limed.* Plot 27. *Unlimed.* Plot 25. *Limed.* Plot 23. *Unlimed.*

Nitrate of Soda. **Sulfate of Ammonia.**

BLUE LUPINE.

All manured alike with potash and phosphoric acid.

from such an admixture, and therefore the figures are the weights for the green material growing upon each narrow row, and, in the case of the above named grasses, the quality of the crop secured from the *nitrate of soda*, plot 27, and the limed plots, 25 and 29, was much superior to that from plot 23.

By comparing the figures in the case of the unlimed plots, we find that *eight* of the varieties produced a heavier yield from *nitrate of soda*, plot 27, and four from sulfate of ammonia, plot 23. Of the varieties of *Agrostis*—red top and Rhode Island bent—two of the four produced their heaviest crop upon plot 23. Their thrifty growth upon this plot, as compared with that of Kentucky blue grass, orchard grass and timothy, showed plainly that they were able to grow upon soils where the conditions were such as to preclude the profitable growth of the last-named grasses.

Turning to the limed plots we find that *here also nitrate of soda gave the greatest total yield in 8 out of the 12 varieties*, and in the other 4 instances the difference in favor of the sulfate of ammonia was slight. In this three year trial with 12 varieties of grasses, *nitrate of soda was*

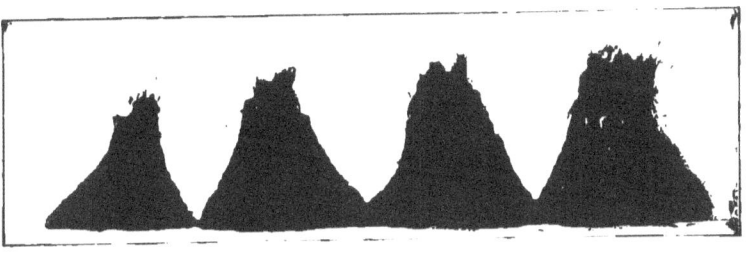

SWEET VERNAL-GRASS.

Plot 23. *Unlimed.* Plot 25. *Limed.* Plot 27. *Unlimed.* Plot 29. *Limed.*
Sulfate of Ammonia. **Nitrate of Soda.**
All manured alike with potash and phosphoric acid.

found to be of superior value, not only in power of production, but in promoting the growth of certain of our most commonly cultivated and most valuable grasses, as timothy, orchard grass and Kentucky blue grass.

NURSERY STOCK.

A limited variety of fruit and shade trees was set on a portion of these plots in the spring of 1896. The stock was selected for the purpose, the trees of each kind as nearly uniform in size and apparent vigor as possible. Any slight differences were equalized, when possible, in dividing up the stock for setting across the four plots. A like number of trees of each kind was set on each plot, and they were pruned in a uniform manner. In 1869 the diameter of each tree was taken with calipers at the beginning and end of the season, and the difference in the measurements showed the growth. The figures given in the table in each case are the average for all the trees of each kind on each plot. The diameters are given in centimeters. The length of new growth was carefully measured, and the average for all the trees of each kind was found for each plot, and is given in inches in the tables. In 1897 it was impracticable to measure the length of new shoots, and the increase in diameter only is given.

A glance at the table will show the *superior effect of nitrate of soda* as compared with sulfate of ammonia, in its influence upon the growth of nursery stock. Many years ago Ruffin, in writing of Virginia soils,

SUNFLOWER.

Plot Nos. 29. Limed.　27 Unlimed.　25. Limed.　23. Unlimed.
Nitrate of Soda.　　**Sulfate of Ammonia.**
All manured alike with Potash and Phosphoric Acid.

and of their improvement through the use of marls, we think called attention to the fact that white birches and yellow pines, when constituting the natural growth upon land, indicate a lack of lime in the soil, *i. e.*, they naturally thrive upon acid soils. We are therefore not surprised to find that the white birch made its best growth in 1896, upon the sulfate of ammonia, although the next year the largest average gain in diameter was made upon the *nitrate of soda*, plot 27, as compared with the sulfate of ammonia, plot 23. In average growth of new wood, in all but 2 instances in the case of the 9 kinds of trees, the *greater growth was made upon the nitrate of soda*, plot 27, as compared with plot 23. Comparing the measurements made upon the limed plots, the greater increase in average diameter was made upon the

TABLE V.

Kinds of Nursery Stock	Year	UNLIMED Plot 23 — Increase in diameter (cm)	UNLIMED Plot 23 — Length of new growth (in)	UNLIMED Plot 27 — Increase in diameter (cm)	UNLIMED Plot 27 — Length of new growth (in)	LIMED Plot 25 — Length of new growth (in)	LIMED Plot 25 — Increase in diameter (cm)	LIMED Plot 29 — Increase in diameter (cm)	LIMED Plot 29 — Length of new growth (in)
American White Birch	1896	0.20	173.25	0.10	129.63	108.71	0.10	0.10	149.46
	1897	0.88		1.00	247.94	243.89	0.56	0.90	293.47
American Elm	1896	0.30	182.89	0.50			0.50	0.60	
	1897	6.90		13.90			15.60	19.30	
American Linden	1896	0.63	31.50	1.18	29.25	57.36	1.54	1.29	74.42
	1897	0.29		0.20			0.10	0.10	
Sugar Maple	1896	0.30	9.17	0.41	10.96	7.42	0.43	0.37	12.61
Orange Quince	1896	0.16	78.55	0.50	151.30	178.85	0.60	0.60	154.55
Bartlett Pear	1896	0.30	43.75	0.50	46.70	50.55	0.64	0.80	57.40
	1897	0.46		0.40			0.40	0.30	
Early Crawford Peach	1896	0.40	324.85	0.68	454.45	588.80	0.72	0.84	488.25
Golden Sweet Apple	1896	1.52	68.15	0.70	84.25	67.30	0.80	0.90	96.75
	1897	0.40		2.66			1.88	2.06	
Baldwin Apple	1896	1.08	81.70	0.40	91.80	75.10	0.40	0.60	77.50
	1897	0.50		1.36			1.10	1.28	
Delaware Grape	1896	1.00	26.90	0.70	49.40	52.65	0.54	0.50	131.00
	1897		30.60	1.68	171.30	328.30	1.34	1.60	423.60
Concord Grape	1896		46.30		126.60	91.80			131.20
	1897		223.20		974.40	918.00			962.00
White Dutch Currant	1896		31.75		45.75	24.32			28.75
Fays' Improved "	1896		27.86		29.58	19.96			36.03

nitrate of soda, plot 29, in 14 out of 17 instances, and the greater average growth of new wood in 11 out of 15 measurements. The latter included every average measurement in the case of the grapes and currants. Before closing with the experiment we wish to notice the yield of small fruits in 1897. The weights are in grams as follows .

SMALL FRUITS, 1897.	UNLIMED.		LIMED.	
	Plot 23. Sulfate of Amm'nia Grams.	Plot 27. Nitrate of Soda. Grams.	Plot 25. Sulfate of Amm'nia Grams.	Plot 29. Nitrate of Soda. Grams.
Strawberries: Lady Rusk.............	62.4	**242.2**	264.9	203.7
" Haverland...............	58.3	**237.6**	370.2	351.1
" Chas. Downing..........	15.2	**351.0**	312.3	**519.3**
Currants: Fay's Prolific.......	9.0	**28.5**	31.5	**89.6**
" White Dutch...............	253.7	**304.5**	281.0	**352.6**
Gooseberry: Smith's Improved.........	88.0	**1428.0**	1505.0	**1614.0**

This experiment has well demonstrated that upon soils which give an acid reaction—and such are far more common than is generally supposed—nitrogen in the form of *nitrate of soda, in connection with phosphoric acid and potash, gives far more profitable returns* than sulfate of ammonia. This fact is attested by the largely increased growth of nearly all of a hundred or more kinds and varieties of field and garden crops, and a large majority of a dozen of the more common grasses and representatives of orchard and fruit trees, grapes and small fruits.

YELLOW CARROT (DANVERS).
Plot Nos. 29. Limed.   27. Unlimed.   25. Limed.   23. Unlimed.
Nitrate of Soda.   **Sulfate of Ammonia.**
All manured alike with Potash and Phosphoric Acid.

It has also shown that the application of air-slaked lime in connection with *nitrate of soda*, potash and phosphoric acid will, upon acid soils, generally render the fertilizers more effective and increase the crops. The plants which are notable exceptions to this rule are the lupines, serradella and watermelon, two varieties of *Agrostis*—red top and Rhode Island bent—and the white birch.

Liming is not particularly injurious to sorrel, as it will thrive upon acid soils, with or without liming, if given an opportunity. The acid condition of some soils forbids the growth of many cultivated plants and grasses, and sorrel comes in naturally to cover the vacant spaces. Liming and the use of *nitrate of soda* tend to correct the acidity, and the soil conditions are changed so that cultivated plants can grow, and sorrel is crowded out.

One great advantage in the use of *nitrate of soda* commonly overlooked is, without doubt, the fact that a basic residue is probably left in the soil when the nitrogen is used by the plant, the tendency of which is, doubtless, to modify soil acidity. On the other hand, the residue from sulfate of ammonia is likely acid in character, and the tendency, therefore, is to aggravate the condition of a soil already acid.

AN EXPERIMENT WITH POTATOES. [1]

In 1896 and 1897 potatoes were grown upon plot 38 for the purpose of testing various combinations of fertilizers, the experiment being in charge of the Director. One of four questions involved was the relative effect of dried blood and *nitrate of soda* as sources of nitrogen for the potato crop. The plot was divided into sections for the experiment, and numbers 1, 3 and 4 were used in this particular inquiry. Like quantities of muriate of potash and dissolved phosphate rock were applied to each section, and equal amounts of nitrogen, in its respective forms, to the several sections. Section 1 received half its nitrogen in the form of dried blood and half in *nitrate of soda*. The following table gives the yields for two years, calculated to bushels per acre :

[1] Tenth Annual Report. R. I. Expt. Station.

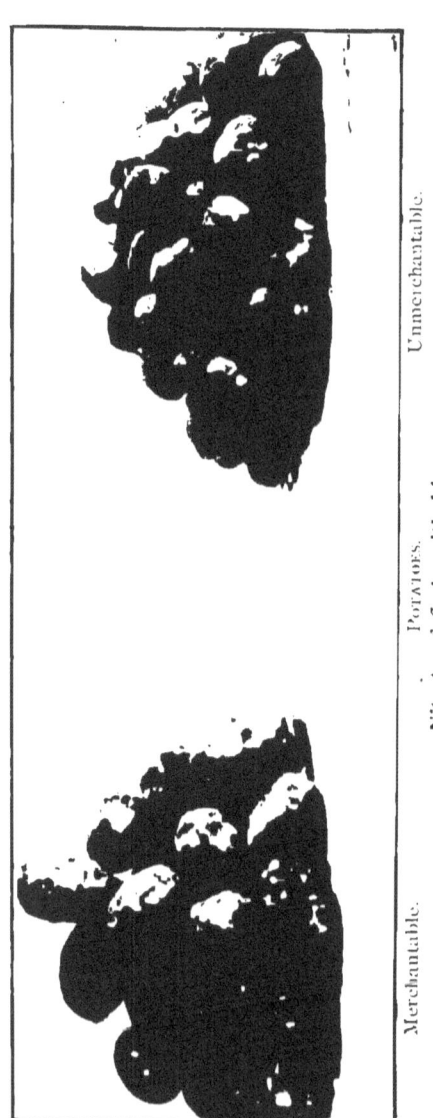

Unmerchantable.

Merchantable.

POTATOES.
Nitrate of Soda with Lime.

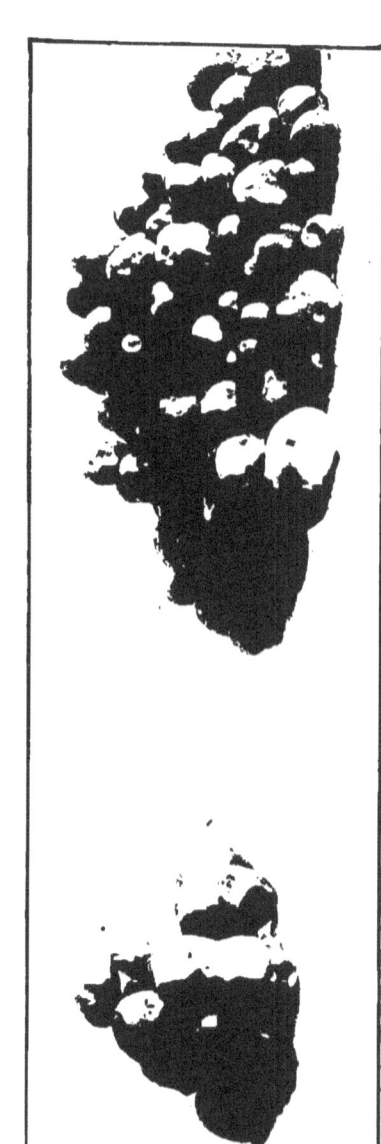

Unmerchantable.

Merchantable.

POTATOES.
Nitrate of Soda without Lime.

POTATO EXPERIMENT, 1896 AND 1897.

No. of Sec- tion	SOURCE OF NITROGEN.	RA- TION	YEAR	YIELDS OF TUBERS IN BUSHELS PER ACRE.		
				Total.	Large.	Small.
1	{ Dried Blood. .... Nitrate of Soda...........	½ } ½ }	1896	289.26	209.75	79.51
1	{ Dried Blood............... Nitrate of Soda	½ } ½ }	1897	246.90	120.96	125.94
	Average,			268.08	165.35	102.72
3	Dried Blood	1	1896	299.78	211.61	88.17
3	" "	1	1897	260.80	127.46	133.34
	Average,			280.29	169.53	110.75
4	Nitrate of Soda	1	1896	302.26	198.00	104.26
4	" " "	1	1897	284.31	148.80	135.51
	Average,			**293.29**	**173.40**	**119.88**

Comparing the average yields for the two years, we find that section 4, the *full ration of nitrate of soda, has given the largest crop :* dried blood, section 3, ranks second ; and the half ration of each. section 3, produced the least.

The average yield from the *full ration* of *nitrate of soda* was *13 bushels* in total crop—3.87 bushels of large potatoes and 9.13 bushels of small ones *more* than the average produced by the full ration of dried blood on section 3.

The average yield from the *full ration* of *nitrate of soda* was *25.21 bushels* in total crop—8.05 bushels of large potatoes and 17.16 bushels of small ones, *more* than the average produced by the half ration each of dried blood and *nitrate of soda* on section 1.

POT EXPERIMENTS.

The following is condensed from an article [1] entitled, " Observations regarding the relative assimilability of various forms of nitrogen upon an acid soil, limed and unlimed," and contains the results of an experiment which was begun in 1893 and continued through 1897.

[1] Tenth Annual Report, R. I. Expt. Station, 1897. pages 241 to 258. By Dr. H. J. Wheeler, B. L. Hartwell and G. E. Adams.

This experiment was conducted in galvanized iron pots or cans, 18 inches in diameter and 26 inches deep, sunk in the soil of a yard made for the purpose. Proper drainage was provided to guard against water flowing into the pots from the outside. In each pot was placed 154 pounds of subsoil and 100 pounds of surface soil taken from plot oo of the co-operative experiment. The soil was a sandy loam with yellow loam subsoil, and it had received no manure whatever for many years. Great care was taken to insure a uniform qual-

SPRING RYE.

Plot Nos. 29. Limed.   27. Unlimed.   25. Limed.   23. Unlimed.

Nitrate of Soda.   **Sulfate of Ammonia.**

All manured alike with Potash and Phosphoric Acid.

ity of soil in all the pots. Like quantities of dissolved bone-black, muriate of potash, and nitrogen in the several forms have been annually added to each pot. Four pots were assigned to each form of nitrogen, two of which were treated, the first year, with air-slaked lime at the rate of 4 tons per acre, and the other two were unlimed. No further application of lime has been made. The dried blood used has been from the same lot, containing 12.45 per cent. of nitrogen. "Pennsylvania tankage," containing 8.9 per cent. of nitrogen, was used in 1893 and 1894, and since then, finely ground leather, containing

7.06 per cent. of nitrogen, has been substituted. Indian corn was raised in 1893, but, owing to the individuality of the plants and the small number which could be grown in each pot, the results were unsatisfactory and the figures are omitted. In 1894 oats were grown. When in the " milk " they were cut, and dried at 100° C. The following table gives the weight for each pot in grams:

OATS.

Plot Nos. 29. Limed. 27. Unlimed.   25. Limed.   23. Unlimed.

Nitrate of Soda.   **Sulfate of Ammonia.**

All manured alike with Potash and Phosphoric Acid.

POT EXPERIMENT.—TABLE I.

OATS, 1894.	No. of Pot.	Limed. Grams per pot.	Unlimed. Grams per pot.
Without Nitrogen	20	....	17.2
	27	....	19.4
	23	55.8	
	24	60.2	....
Nitrate of Soda	6		59.4
	13	....	69.9
	7	78.6	
	14	69.9	....
Sulfate of Ammonia	18	....	7.1
	25	....	14.0
	19	72.9	
	26	83.1	....
Dried Blood	4	....	58.9
	11	....	50.3
	5	67.9	
	12	68.1	....
"Pennsylvania Tankage"	2	....	45.7
	9	....	47.3
	3	73.1	....
	10	76.5	....

In the case of the *unlimed* plots, *nitrate of soda* produced considerably *better results* than any other form of nitrogen.

In 1895 spring rye was sown, harvested in the "milk," and dried at 100° C. The weight in grams per pot was as follows :

POT EXPERIMENT.—TABLE II.

SPRING RYE, 1895.	No. of Pot.	LIMED. Grams per pot.	UNLIMED. Grams per pot.
Without Nitrogen	20		4.2
	27	. . .	3.8
	23	56.7	. . .
	24	44.6	. . .
Nitrate of Soda	6	. . .	22.7
	13	. . .	24.5
	7	118.7	
	14	93.6	. . .
Sulfate of Ammonia.	18	. . .	0.6
	25	. . .	1.0
	19	108.4	
	26	97.5	. . .
Dried Blood.	4		1.0
	11	. . .	1.7
	5	117.6	. . .
	12	100.5	. . .
Ground Leather	2		3.9
	9	. . .	8.9
	3	64.9	
	10	76.3	

"The superiority of nitrate of soda as a form of nitrogen for acid soils is again strikingly manifested."

RESULTS WITH BARLEY IN 1896.

"For the reason that plants of the same kind, weighing exactly alike, may contain unlike amounts of nitrogen, and since the actual amount of nitrogen in plants is dependent, within certain limits, upon the quantity of that element present in assimilable form within the soil, the quantities of nitrogen removed from the soil by the crop have, in most cases, been determined. By this means, much more reliable information is furnished as to the relative assimilability of the several forms of nitrogenous manures."

NITRATE OF SODA

POT EXPERIMENT.—TABLE III.

BARLEY, 1896.	Pot No.	Limed.			Unlimed.		
		Grams of barley hay per pot.	Per cent. of nitrogen in the crop (fully dried).	Grams of nitrogen obtained from the soil by the crop.	Grams of barley hay per pot.	Per cent. of nitrogen in the crop (fully dried).	Grams of nitrogen obtained from the soil by the crop.
Without Nitrogen	20	....		.....	9.61	1.75	0.168
	27	....	....	.....	8.18	1.14	0.093
	23	58.67	1.14	0.791	....	....	.....
	24	69.26	1.00	0.693	....	....	.....
Nitrate of Soda	6	....	....	.....	51.07	2.29	1.170
	13	....	....	.....	51.12	2.43	1.242
	7	100.32	2.17	2.177	....	....	.....
	14	103.56	2.07	2.144	....	....	.....
Sulfate of Ammonia	18	....	....		*	*	*
	25	....	....	.....	2.46	*	*
	19	102.48	2.00	2.050	....	....	.....
	26	98.78	1.66	1.646	....	....	.....
Dried Blood	4	....	....	.....	21.26	2.32	0.493
	11	....	....	.....	32.85	2.27	0.746
	5	118.21	1.73	2.045	....	....	.....
	12	120.52	1.66	2.000	....	....	.....
Ground Leather	2	....	....		11.20	1.89	0.212
	9	....	....	.....	11.71	2.06	0.241
	3	73.90	1.23	0.909	....	....	
	10	79.14	1.22	0.966	....	....	

* Not determined, owing to small amount of substance.

In the limed series it will be seen that, so far as concerns the weight of dry matter in the crop, dried blood proved superior to either sulfate of ammonia or *nitrate of soda*, yet the plants receiving *nitrate of soda actually removed the larger amount of nitrogen from the soil*. In this instance the weight of the crop fails to indicate properly the relative assimilability of the nitrogen of the dried blood and the *nitrate of soda*.

Dried blood in the unlimed series exceeded leather in yield and amount of nitrogen removed. "*Nitrate of soda* as a source of nitrogen on an acid soil *has again shown its marked superiority, the total product of barley hay, and the amount of nitrogen removed being far greater in the case of those pots than in any of the others*.

Deducting the amount of nitrogen found in the crop from the

POT EXPERIMENT.—TABLE IV.

BARLEY, 1897.	Pot No.	LIMED.			UNLIMED.		
		Grams of barley hay per pot.	Per cent. of nitrogen in the crop (fully dried).	Grams of nitrogen obtained from the soil by the crop.	Grams of barley hay per pot.	Per cent. of nitrogen in the crop (fully dried).	Grams of nitrogen obtained from the soil by the crop.
Without Nitrogen.	20	....			4.69	1	1
	27	....	...	....	2.40	1	1
	23	32.79	1	1	....		
	24	27.19	1	1	....		
Nitrate of Soda.	6	....	....	....	42.33	2.01	0.851
	13	....	....	....	28.24	2.02	0.570
	7	80.37	2.02	1.623	....	....	....
	14	75.86	1.91	1.449	....	...	....
Sulfate of Ammonia	18	....	....	....	2	2	2
	25	....	....	....	1.23	1	1
	19	79.96	1.76	1.407	....	....	....
	26	61.95	1.89	1.171	....	....	....
Dried Blood.	4	....	....	....	12.31	1.95	0.240
	11	....	....	....	3	3	3
	5	85.37	1.60	1.366	....	....	....
	12	87.26	1.67	1.457	....	....	....
Ground Leather.	2	....	....	....	8.06	1.67	0.135
	9	....	....	....	9.74	1.60	0.156
	3	30.45	1.55	0.466	....	....	....
	10	40.96	1.26	0.516	....	....	....

[1] Not determined, owing to small amount of substance.
[2] This pot received caustic magnesia in 1896 and 1897, and results are reserved for publication elsewhere.
[3] Waterlogged.

pots without nitrogen, from that in the pots when nitrogen was added, and then letting 100 represent the average amount of nitrogen taken from the soil by the plants in the *nitrate of soda* pots, we obtain the following values for the nitrogen, which the plants were able to obtain from the other forms of nitrogen employed.

	LIMED.		UNLIMED.	
	Pots.	Average.	Pots.	Average.
Nitrate of Soda	23. 24	100.0	20. 27	100.0
Sulfate of Ammonia	19. 26	92.2	— —	—
Dried Blood	5. 12	90.3	4. 11	45.5
Ground Steamed Leather	3. 10	13.8	2. 9	0.9

"These results bring out plainly the fact that upon an acid soil, where nitrification progresses but slowly, much of the money invested in the best forms of organic nitrogen, such as blood, meat and fish, is practically wasted; and since these forms make up the major part of the nitrogen of most of the commercial fertilizers sold in the state, the importance of testing the soils for acidity, and of supplying lime where needed, cannot be too strongly insisted upon."

BARLEY.
Plot Nos. 29. Limed. 27. Unlimed.   25. Limed. 23. Unlimed.
Nitrate of Soda.   **Sulfate of Ammonia.**
All manured alike with Potash and Phosphoric Acid.

The *superiority of nitrate of soda as a source of nitrogen over organic forms* could hardly be more clearly demonstrated. On a well-limed soil it is shown to furnish nearly *8 per cent. more available nitrogen* than sulfate of ammonia, and about *10 per cent. more* than good dried blood. In the case of an acid unlimed soil, it is practically *100 per cent. more profitable* to use than sulfate of ammonia or steamed leather, and furnishes *54.5 per cent. more* available nitrogen than dried blood.

SUGGESTIONS REGARDING THE USE OF NITRATE OF SODA AND LIME.

NITRATE OF SODA is valuable as a fertilizer upon any soil in field, garden or greenhouse, in which additional nitrogen is required for maximum plant growth, and when, for any reason, a soil is acid, it becomes probably the most efficient form of nitrogenous material to apply. This is, doubtless, because of the fact that what remains in the soil after the nitrogen is used by plant growth seems, in a measure, to neutralize the soil acidity and thereby give better conditions for the thrifty growth of most agricultural plants. Soils upon which clover and timothy fail to make a "catch" when sown, and where red-top (*Agrostis vulgaris*) quickly takes the place of timothy, and forms the bulk of the hay crop ; soils where the cultivated grasses soon die out and give place to wild grasses, rushes and sorrel ; soils where wheat and barley fail to thrive, and soils where beets, spinach and lettuce fail altogether, or make but a feeble growth, *are most probably acid*, and should be promptly tested for acidity. If a soil is acid when tested, changing a blue litmus paper to a reddish color sometimes approaching a brick-red—it is economy to use some other agent in addition to *nitrate of soda* for correcting the acid condition.

The most convenient and, generally, cheaper materials for this purpose are air-slaked lime and wood ashes, both leached and unleached. The fact that applications of wood ashes often show a marked effect for many years is, doubtless, due to the influence of the thirty or more per cent. of carbonate of lime which they contain, along with other carbonates, all of which neutralize acidity and help to promote nitrification in acid soils deficient in lime. One ton per acre of air-slaked lime is capable of producing surprising results when used with other fertilizers upon acid soils, and the *application of lime has to be made but once in several years*. In connection with the " Phosphate experiment" at the Rhode Island Agricultural Experiment Station,[1] upon a sandy loam soil, so acid and infertile that without lime or fertilizers Indian corn will not grow more than from *four to six inches high*, one ton of air-slaked lime per acre, applied in 1894, and annual applications of nitrate of soda and muriate of potash, with suitable quantities of phosphoric acid in different forms, but *no further application of lime*, has produced an increase in the total hay crop of 1896–97 and the first crop of 1898, of 8889 pounds of hay, as compared with the total yield from the unlimed plots. This gain of practically *four and a half tons* of hay per acre in three years is the direct result of the application of one ton of air-slaked lime in 1894. In addition to increase in quantity, the *quality* of the hay from the limed plots has been superior to that from those unlimed.

SEEDING TO GRASS.

This is probably the best time in the rotation to apply lime or ashes. If the latter are used, about 100 bushels, or two tons per acre, should be applied ; spread them evenly, and work them well into the soil. If lime is used, one to two tons per acre is generally sufficient. Too much lime may be as injurious as too little. If purchased as a waste product already slaked, spread evenly upon the field, and work into the soil by thorough harrowing. If purchased in the caustic, or freshly-burned state, haul to the field and place in heaps of about one half barrel each at proper distances over the field. With a watering-pot spray about one and a quarter pails of water upon each heap, and cover with a few shovel-fulls of moist earth. In one or two days the heaps will have slaked to a fine dry powder, which can best be spread from a scoop-shovel. Select, if possible, a time when there is no wind to interfere with the spreading, but it is desirable to spread it and harrow it in before any heavy rain falls. If any lumps remain unslaked, and the field is to be immediately seeded, they should be gathered up and removed, as, otherwise, they would be slaked by the first fall of rain, and, thereby, kill all the seed in the vicinity of each lump, though it be no larger than a hickory-nut. If the lime can be spread, harrowed in, and the seeding postponed until after a good rain has fallen, all small lumps will then have become slaked, and the lime more thoroughly incorporated with the soil by the additional

---

[1] See Annual Reports for 1896 and 1897.

cultivation. Caustic lime increases in weight about 27.5 per cent. by dry-slaking with a small quantity of water. When eight barrels of caustic lime, 250 pounds net each, are used per acre, the dressing is equivalent to one and a quarter tons of air-slaked lime.

If phosphoric acid in some insoluble form, as fine ground bone, slag meal, or floats is used in the fertilizer, it is doubtless best to make a liberal application at time of seeding, and to confine the subsequent top-dressing mainly to applications of potash and nitrate of soda ; but if soluble phosphates are used, as dissolved bone-black, dissolved bone, or dissolved phosphate rock, a lighter application should be made at seeding-time, especially if done in the autumn, and then phosphoric acid should be regularly included in the spring top-dressing. If seeding is done in the early fall, and the soil has been tolerably well fertilized for previous crops, so as to be in good condition, either of the following formulas may be used :

FALL SEEDING NO. 1.

Nitrate of Soda............. 50 to 100 pounds per acre.
Muriate of Potash.......... 50 to 100   "   "
Fine ground Bone ....400 to 600   "   "

Slag meal (Thomas slag) 600 to 800 pounds, or floats (raw phosphate rock finely ground) 800 to 1000 pounds may be used in place of the fine ground bone with about equally good effect. Each spring, following the seeding, just after the grass begins to start into growth, the following top-dressing should be applied :

Nitrate of Soda ....130 pounds per acre.
Muriate of Potash 100   "   "

If the field is kept in grass more than three years, about 300 pounds of dissolved bone-black, or its equivalent in dissolved phosphate rock or dissolved bone, should be regularly added to the spring top-dressing. The above formula can be equally well used for spring seeding, although in the latter case the nitrate of soda and muriate of potash should be increased by the amount used in the spring top-dressing.

If soluble phosphates are used, and the seeding is done in the early fall, the following formula will do good service :

FALL SEEDING NO. 2.

Nitrate of Soda............. 50 to 100 pounds per acre.
Muriate of Potash.......... 50 to 100   "   "
Dissolved Bone-Black ....150 to 250   "   "

From 200 to 300 pounds of dissolved phosphate rock may be substituted for the bone-black if found to cost less. If the above formula is used, the following top-dressing should be applied each spring when the growth of grass begins :

Nitrate of Soda ....120 pounds per acre.
Muriate of Potash................120   "   "
Dissolved Bone-Black or Phosphate
  Rock 300   "   "

Formula No. 2 may be used for spring seeding by adding to it the top-dressing intended for spring application.

WINTER WHEAT.

If the soil is acid, lime should be applied as for seeding to grass, and

Fine Ground Bone..........300 to 400 pounds per acre,
or Dissolved Phosphate Rock ..200 to 300   "   "

used at time of seeding. In the spring, top-dress with 120 pounds of nitrate of soda per acre. If the soil is known to be deficient in potash, 120 pounds of muriate of potash should be applied at time of sowing.

WINTER RYE.

The same fertilizer may be used for rye as for wheat, except that rye is less dependent upon the lime than is wheat. Rye can withstand the unfavorable conditions of an acid soil fairly well, and will generally produce a crop, especially if top-dressed in early spring with 120 pounds of nitrate of soda per acre.

OATS.

The following formula has been used for the oat crop, in connection with the "rotations," at the Rhode Island Experiment Station :

Nitrate of Soda.............. ....200 pounds per acre.
Dissolved Phosphate Rock 176   "   "
Fine Ground Bone 180   "   "
Muriate of Potash 120   "   "

The above should give a good crop upon soil of moderate quality.

BARLEY AND BEETS.

The following formula has been used upon acid soils, in connection with work performed by the Rhode Island Experiment Station in different parts of the State. In each case the soil received, in addition, a dressing of two and a half tons of air-slaked lime per acre

Nitrate of Soda.................300 pounds per acre.
Muriate of Potash 300   "   "
Dissolved Bone-Black 900   "   "

The equivalent of the bone-black in dissolved phosphate rock might frequently be more economical.

MANGELS AFTER CLOVER.

This land was limed at the rate of two and a half tons per acre, previous to seeding to clover. *Lime* should *always* be used upon acid soils before attempting to grow beets of any variety.

Nitrate of Soda..................360 pounds per acre.
Dissolved Phosphate Rock.........840   "   "
Muriate of Potash................300   "   "

PEAS.

The following formula has produced good crops of peas in one of the rotations at the Rhode Island Experiment Station :

Nitrate of Soda ....120 pounds per acre.
Dissolved Phosphate Rock 397   "   "
Muriate of Potash 135   "   "

GARDEN CROPS AND VINES.

Nitrate of Soda............... .. 450 pounds per acre.
Fine Ground Bone...............500   "   "
Dissolved Phosphate Rock 500   "   "
Muriate of Potash 300   "   "

When successive crops are grown upon the same land in one season, additional applications of fertilizer will be required. Top-dressing all crops valued for the leaf growth, as cabbage, celery, lettuce, etc., with *nitrate of soda* will greatly increase the growth.

TURNIPS.

Nitrate of Soda ....120 pounds per acre.
Dissolved Phosphate Rock.... ...331   "   "
Fine Ground Bone....... 240   "   "
Muriate of Potash 150   "   "

ASPARAGUS.

This plant fails, or produces but a feeble growth, upon an acid soil without lime. Two tons, or more, per acre of air-slaked lime can be safely applied if a soil shows much acidity.

Nitrate of Soda.................450 pounds per acre.
Dissolved Phosphate Rock.........500   "   "
Fine Ground Bone.................400   "   "
Muriate of Potash 300   "   "

If the soil is deficient in potash, the quantity used in the formula should be considerably increased. One half of this fertilizer may be applied and worked into the soil in the early spring, and the remainder, just before cutting ceases, and the permanent summer growth begins. A vigorous growth of top through the summer and fall is desirable, as the roots are then prepared to send up an abundant crop of shoots the following spring.

INDIAN CORN, No. 1.

Nitrate of Soda ....225 pounds per acre.
Dissolved Phosphate Rock 420   "   "
Fine Ground Bone.................150   "   "
Muriate of Potash 120   "   "

INDIAN CORN, No. 2.

Muriate of Potash............   180 pounds per acre.
Dissolved Phosphate Rock.........550   "   "
Nitrate of Soda 250   "   "

IRISH POTATOES.

The fertilizer used in growing potatoes upon plot 38, in a fertilizer experiment with potatoes at the Rhode Island Experiment Station, was composed of the following :

Nitrate of Soda.... ....344 pounds per acre.
Dissolved Phosphate Rock.........875   "   "
Muriate of Potash 215   "   "

On many soils, high grade sulfate of potash in place of the muriate would probably give an equally good crop, and the quality of the tubers might be better. *Lime should not be used* with, or just preceding, the potato crop, for, although it has a tendency to slightly increase the crop, and especially the proportion of marketable tubers, the neutral or alkaline condition of the soil, which it creates, is highly favorable to the development of the "scab" fungus, and a "scabby" crop is likely to follow its use. If the "scab" germ is *not present in the soil*, and the seed tubers are so *thoroughly disinfected* that it is *not introduced* upon them, then potatoes may be safely grown upon freshly-limed land.

The formulas given above are not intended as "hard and fast rules" under all circumstances, but as suggestions which the prudent cultivator may safely adapt to his individual circumstances.

Nitrate of soda usually furnishes from 15 to 16 per cent. of nitrogen, *i. e.*, 15 to 16 pounds in every 100 pounds of material. Muriate of potash yields about 50 per cent. of actual potash. The phosphatic materials are much more variable in composition, but dissolved bone-black contains, generally, from 15 to 16 per cent. of available phosphoric acid ; dissolved phosphate rock about 13 per cent., although different lots may vary from 11 to 17 per cent., of available phosphoric acid. Fine ground bone has about 2 per cent. of nitrogen and some 20 to 27 per cent of total phosphoric acid ; slag meal, about 18 per cent. of total phosphoric acid, and floats, about 26 per cent. In preparing the foregoing formulas, the relative cost and efficiency of the phosphatic materials, as well as the actual content of phosphoric acid, has been considered.

For full information in regard to Nitrate of
Soda as a Fertilizer apply to address below. All
publications furnished free.

PROPAGANDA FOR NITRATE OF SODA,

12 JOHN STREET,

NEW YORK CITY.

INDEX.

LIST OF CUTS.